Lions in Winter

Wena Poon was born in Singapore and moved to the United States when she was seventeen. Her fiction and poetry have been widely published and, as a freelance journalist, she wrote for publications such as *Film Quarterly*, *Marie Claire* and *The Straits Times*. In 2008, *Lions In Winter* was listed for the International Frank O'Connor Award in Ireland and the Singapore Literature Prize. She holds degrees in English Literature and Law from Harvard and is a practising attorney.

WENA POON

lions in winter

SALT

LONDON

PUBLISHED BY SALT PUBLISHING
Fourth Floor, 2 Tavistock Place, Bloomsbury, London WC1H 9RA United Kingdom
All rights reserved

First published by Salt Publishing 2009

Printed and bound in the United Kingdom by MPG Books Group

Typeset in Swift 11 / 14

ISBN 978 1 84471 576 3 paperback

1 3 5 7 9 8 6 4 2

To my grandmother, Yeo Ah Siak, the first raconteur I knew.

CONTENTS

lions
in
winter

PREFACE

In Singapore, someone who leaves the country is said to have "migrated". Ours is a sparse language—evidently, nobody saw the need to say "emigrated". Too many syllables. But more importantly, the emphasis is on the idea of *migration*—to leave and settle down elsewhere, never to return.

In mainland China, they call people who leave China *hai gui*, which is translated roughly as "overseas-return". They are the "returnees"— young Chinese men and women who go to the West for a college degree and then come back to build their society. It is a word pun, for it also means "sea turtle."

Sea turtles don't migrate. They exhibit *philopatry*, from the Greek philo ("love") and patris ("fatherland"). They hatch, swim out into the wild tides of the vast ocean, and come back from time to time to their old nesting grounds.

I migrated from Singapore to the United States when I was 17, leaving one of England's smallest former colonies for her largest. Despite liking the rough tumble of ocean waves, I regularly swim back for the shore. I have been a little philopatric.

During my travels, I began writing a series of love letters—masquerading as short stories—to Singapore. Written in the English language, they were published by Asian literary journals and anthologies and eventually collected in book form by MPH, a Malaysian publisher, in 2007.

The Salt edition is the first time these stories are reaching the wider English-reading public. Although written for my compatriots, these stories have appealed to people of different nationalities and ethnicities. If you are not living in the small town or even the country of your birth— and especially if you display philopatric tendencies—I hope you enjoy this volume. Leaving, after all, is never really goodbye.

WENA POON, Austin, Texas
September 2009

xi

ADDICTION

HE WROTE THE WORD on the very first page of the new notebook he had purchased from Liberty's on Regent Street. He watched as the ink sank gently into the creamy smooth paper.

It was a strange word. If you stared at it long enough, you started doubting if it was actually spelled that way. Weren't there too many "d"s?

Addiction.

When he first came to England, he had a thick Singaporean accent. Over time, he sanded it down patiently until it lost its outlines and merged into the pea soup mix of London accents that the immigrant community—including the Tibetan carpet-seller downstairs—had acquired.

A "faint British accent." A decision to pronounce vowels long rather than short, like they did in America. When he first came to England, he had difficulty pronouncing the word "edited." He worked in the student newspaper, and they used to laugh.

"I edited your piece yesterday," he would say.

"Eh-dited! Eh-dited!" laughed the reporter. "Not uh-dit-ed! It sounds like you're addicted to something."

The professor in a poetry class he had attended said it was difficult for Alistair to grasp things like iambic pentameter.

"It is a curiosity among the Singaporean and Malaysian students," said Professor Henley. "They can never hear the beat. Ta-dum, ta-dum, ta-dum. They pronounce all the words with an even stress on every syllable."

Yeah, thanks for referring to me in the third person, right in front of me, scowled Alistair, writing the word again and again on the page.

Addiction. Ah-*dick*-shion.

1

Well, he took care of his accent. He was shy; he didn't want to stand out in London. He felt that as long as he spoke with his native accent, the people in London would never get over it so as to actually hear what he was saying. And he had a lot to say, a lot to do, during his time there. So he practiced. If Gwyneth Paltrow could do it, so could he. He spent long evenings shut up in his room in the bedsit, reading out passages from Charles Dickens, imitating all the voices in the dialogue parts. When he got excited, his accent slipped back to Singaporean, but otherwise he was able to maintain an even keel on the British accent. A curious thing, the Singaporean accent. Back in Singapore, he felt sorry for the newscasters who seemed to be fighting, with each enunciated word, an inner battle of epic proportions. To be true to oneself, and speak like everybody else on the street, or to fake a British accent. They always compromised horribly.

When Alistair spoke to his parents, or when he was back in Singapore, he reverted to his Singaporean accent. His parents must not suspect that he had changed in any way. His parents called him regularly, every Saturday. They said his sister was getting married. Super achiever Yvette was going to marry this lawyer kid from Cambridge.

"His father works for the Chief Justice of Singapore," said his mum.

"So? His father isn't the Chief Justice," said Alistair.

"Yes, but he *works for* the Chief Justice."

Alistair marveled at his middle class family's complicated schemes for social advancement.

"Why don't you just cut to the chase and have Yvette marry the Chief Justice himself?"

"You are always talking nonsense. Your father is asking, how are your medical studies?"

"Fine."

"When are you going to send your report card home?"

"Mum, there is no 'report card' for you to sign, I'm not a kid anymore." Alistair was exasperated. His parents never made it past secondary school; when referring to his university life, they still used words like "report card" and "principal" and "teacher".

"I just want to make sure you are doing well, because we paid that seventy-five *kay* bond for you to the Singapore government," said his mum. She liked to say "kay" for "thousand". As in, "I paid two *kay* for that diamond ring." It was a habit that irritated him. It was a sign of barbarism, he decided. A barbaric attitude towards money, that reduced something vast to a small, inconsequential syllable.

She wanted him to be back for the holidays. He braced himself for their usual fight, but this time she introduced a new controversy. He had just met up with her friend's daughter two days ago. Aunty Somebody's sister's daughter's ex-schoolmate, who was also studying in London. Because of the prevailing belief that young Singaporeans who happen to be studying in the same town must naturally want to meet up, his mother suggested that the girl call on him at his bedsit, which he rented from an elderly English couple. Alistair proposed that they meet at Starbucks, but it was overruled. His mother wanted the girl to visit his flat. There was something illicit about the way his mother forced the girl upon her. Later, he realized why. The girl reported back to his mother. She had been sent as a spy.

"She says your flat smells of smoke. And marijuana."

Alistair did not respond immediately. Then he laughed.

"Oh my God! How does she know what marijuana smells like? I don't even know."

"That's what I thought," said his mother brightly. "I thought more likely she was using it herself, the silly slut! Accusing my son of dabbling in drugs." The penalty for the possession of marijuana in Singapore was death; it was an unknown quotient in that country. Ecstasy, yes. Marijuana, hash, cocaine, no. The stubborn minority of society that in the West has always used recreational drugs since (and before) Thomas de Quincey wrote *Confessions of an Opium Eater* did not exist in Singapore. Look into the dark corners, and you will find nothing, thought Alistair. Drugs were not a big issue. Sex was not a big issue. A lot of things were just—blip, zilch, zero. Never arose in normal conversation. Don't go there. Ain't happening. Nope.

He took out his usual plastic bag of grass.

3

"The smoke comes in from the flat next door. A bunch of English guys, they smoke a lot. Comes in from under the door." He rolled a spliff and lit it. He smoked and listened as his mother droned on.

"What kind of people do you live next door to? Criminals? Prostitutes?"

He assured her that his building in Islington was crammed full of respectable folk. His landlord was a retired firefighter and his wife volunteered at the church. That seemed to calm his mother down. She was not Christian, but she had a very Chinese respect for Western institutionalized religion, which she associated with great self-cultivation and learning. Her distrust of white people could often be tempered down if Alistair chose to say that they were "good Christians." Unfortunately, it was too late for him to redeem his grass-smoking neighbors.

"You better be careful, Alistair. I heard that it is highly dangerous to even inhale marijuana smoke from someone else. Even if they are next door, you might become addicted!" his mother fretted. "That's why your father is so worried about you being over there by yourself. We can't watch over you. You're a boy, so we're not as worried about you as when Yvette went over there, but you have to be extra careful. Lock your door at night, and don't get into lifts with any whites or blacks."

That would mean never ever getting to use any lifts, he thought. He told her not to worry and listened to her plans for a party to celebrate his next visit to Singapore. He was tired, and he still had to finish his student project. He dug his mobile phone out of his pocket and called his own telephone number. When the beeps came through, he said, "Oops, I have to go. Someone's calling in."

"Who is calling so late?"

Alistair drew a deep hit and considered.

"Mum, you know I share this phone with my landlord. It might be someone for them."

She relented and hung up. Until next week, Mum, he thought silently. He looked at the telephone, hating it. The telephone was a tool

4

of oppression, a long-distance cudgel that his parents used to remind him that he may be far away but was not yet free. He thought about changing the number. It had grown so bad that the skin at the back of his neck would tingle whenever it rang. His heart would race. If he did-n't pick it up, his mother would go berserk. Horrible thoughts would crowd her vision. Once, she said she contacted the London police because she had called and called and left many messages over the course of a day but couldn't get hold of him. It was when he was over at Brian's flat. That had been a horrible day, and of course the last thing he wanted to do was to talk to his parents. He had fallen into a hole so deep, he was lying in Brian's bed, crying his heart out into the dark blue flannel sheets. He was in a place where nobody, not even Brian, could touch, let alone his parents. The thought of their utter irrele-vance to his problems made him cry even harder.

"I just can't do it anymore, man," said Brian. "I'm broke. It's too damn expensive in London."

"I could get a job up north," said Alistair.

"What about school? You're graduating next year."

"I can transfer."

"Forget it, you're in the best design school in Britain. You're going to make it big, Alistair. You might get hired by a big shot. What are you going to design in Manchester? Football uniforms?" Brian stroked his head. "You can come visit me anytime. You know where my old man lives."

But for a long time, Alistair lay naked in bed, refusing to get up. He couldn't believe that they had just discussed breaking up. He watched as Brian pulled on his favorite T-shirt, some obscure northern band that Alistair had never heard of. He called it Brian's "stupid band T-shirt".

Later, when hunger got the better of them, they went to a somber little Chinese restaurant round the corner. They were the only cus-tomers.

"You ever heard of Annabelle Chong?" asked Alistair.

Brian shook his head.

5

"She starred in some big gang-bang movie. She broke records for having sex with the most men."

"So?"

"She's from my sister Yvette's high school in Singapore. Sweet kid. Came over here, got gang-raped. Big shame, couldn't tell her parents, couldn't face her society. Ended up being the biggest Asian porn star in cinematic history."

"God."

Alistair laughed mirthlessly. "I feel like her sometimes."

Brian smiled and gave him a shove under the table. "What, like I gang-banged you? You going to be a porn star?"

"No. Not quite. I mean I can probably see how she just ended up, you know," Alistair's voice trailed off as he looked out at the traffic beyond the windows of the restaurant. "Spiraling down."

❧

When he realized, two months into the term, that there was no way he was going to study medicine, he switched to textile and fashion design. A year later, at the encouragement of his professor, he transferred himself out of the university that his parents thought he was enrolled in, and got into the top fashion design college in London. He was the only Asian student in his program, and for all he knew the only Singaporean who ever made it this far. Unlike Yvette's honors from Cambridge in Law, however, Alistair's advancement could not be made known to his parents, and could not be celebrated. There were only two professions that the Tan family thought was suitable for their children: being a doctor, or a lawyer. Men who went into fashion, whether as models or designers, were *Ah Kwa*, the Chinese epithet for "transvestite." As a Chinese man you were not required to be particularly macho—there were few expectations of great physical strength or an excellence in sports—but swing too far in the other direction, and you might as well have had a sex change operation.

There was an *Ah Kwa* in Alistair's extended family, a distant relative.

The man's family refused to speak to him and claimed that his condition was caused by a swimming accident in which he nearly drowned. "The shock was too much," said Alistair's mother by way of explanation whenever the topic arose. "It affected his brain."

When Alistair left Singapore, his parents had cautioned him, "Don't associate too much with white people. They are all addicted to sex and drugs. London in particular is full of *Ah Kwas*. Be careful, otherwise they will drag you into their habits. You will be influenced." His mother would have loved to seal Alistair up in a Zip-Loc bag before exporting him if she could, so that he did not bring home any nasty influences. As much as she loved to tell her relatives that her son was studying in the UK, it was expected that he was only to bring home the prestigious title of a UK medical degree, and none of the "other stuff": drugs, sex, homosexuality, divorces.

Ah Kwa, wrote Alistair in his notebook. Or was it spelled, *Ah Gua*? Then, under it, he wrote, *dirty. Dirty Dirty Dirty*.

At his first fashion show, Alistair bungled horribly. They were asked to explore a personal theme. Alistair naively drew from his heritage. He hand-dyed batiks in plastic buckets in his tiny bedroom and bathroom for weeks. His landlord was unhappy. His nails were permanently dyed red, like those of a Malay bride.

When the day came, he watched his models parade down the catwalk in his batik designs, and was overwhelmed with anger. He was stupid, stupid, thinking he could pander to his Asian background. They just looked like cocktail waitresses. They looked like air stewardesses. His designs looked cheap. He saw what the other students had designed. There was nothing he could design that could beat the sheer, studied sophistication of what they were doing. He felt he could never catch up.

Once again he resented the pretty little world in which he had grown up. The flat symmetry of Singapore; the clever, cautious people. None of his London classmates were pretend medical students. Many, in fact, came from artistic backgrounds. One of them was the son of Lady Somebody or other, who had been a powerful editor at British

Vogue in the fifties. The boy grew up in a mansion with rose trellises in Barbados and collected eighteenth-century French antiques. Alistair grew up in a public housing estate in Singapore and did not see the inside of a museum until he was sixteen. His parents' idea of style was non-crinkle polyester clothes from Japanese department stores. He was light years behind, he told himself furiously.

And yet he always had an innate sense of style. As a child, against the wishes of his parents, he had drawn and drawn and excelled in art classes. His parents accused him of being a "dreamer." He had an instinctive grasp of the human form and its infinite variations. Above all, he had always been in love with painting and sculpture. He gravitated towards Western art because he never saw much Asian art growing up. It was a question of exposure. When he visited Paris with his parents, he clamored to see the Louvre. His parents waited for him at the gift shop, then derided him petulantly for wanting to see so many paintings of "naked women."

"Now I know why you want to come here," said his father, holding up a guide book of the Louvre's collection. The cover showed a seventeenth century painting of the Muses, their breasts bared. His father said in Chinese dialect, in case the other tourists heard: "These Western women, they always had great tits, huh?"

Alistair was utterly humiliated. Little blue-frocked French schoolgirls trickled past him on their day trip to the museum, listening to their enthusiastic teacher go on about the life of Eugene Delacroix. His mother was tight-lipped and said that young children should not be exposed to so much nudity. "Look at our Chinese art," she said to no one in particular.

In London, Alistair put up a huge poster of the Sistine Chapel ceiling over his bed. He went to sleep among Michelangelo's sybils. He wanted to design something that was completely celebratory of the physical form. He went to the British Museum and pondered among Venuses. So much of what he saw in other students' designs was bitter. Bitter, holocaustic, self-referential, deconstructive. He had to do something different. When he slept, he dreamed hard.

In the end, Alistair chose happiness. He sent out his models in diaphanous silk dresses, each painstakingly micro-pleated so that they clung, sinuously, to breasts and hips. All the dresses were soft pink. The straps and buckles were made with silver thread and hand-sewn paste diamonds. His models went barefooted. He called the collection *Iphigenia at Aulis*. He created an uproar. "Flapper meets Grecian wood nymph," said the student newspaper. His faculty advisers were happy: "Beautifully sewn. Well done." The models were happy. They wanted to keep the dresses. They begged. He met a buyer from Brown's, and he hadn't even graduated.

He met Brian, who worked at a nearby student pub. They started going to a lot of museums together, because it was free and because London was cold. Brian played the electric guitar and wrote music. They collaborated for one of the student shows. They didn't get paid, but got good reviews.

Alistair couldn't remember when he realized he was gay, only that he was surprised that he didn't feel uncomfortable when he fell in love. The rest was easy. When you are in love with someone, bodies fall away. It was not true that you would always get hurt when you are naked, he thought. He never thought about telling his parents. After all, they always pretended they never had sex, that he and his sister came by stork. They belonged to a different world. He didn't tell his sister, Yvette, because he knew she would make him feel ashamed. She was the kind of Singaporean girl who put the name of her church on her C.V. It was important that one went to the right country club; the right church. But even at the right church, things happen. Someone at her church came out of the closet years ago. Big story. Their parents took out an advertisement in the papers disclaiming future family ties with their son. The pastor prepared a special sermon.

"I cannot fucking believe it," said Brian, looking at him with serious dark eyes. "An advert in a paper, you say."

"I guess I don't care," said Alistair, gluing another paste diamond on a sandal. "But I just don't want to cause any trouble. I just can't stand drama. Here, are you going to help me or not? I'll never finish these sandals in time."

Brian helped him cut designs, bead borders, mix dyes. When winter came, they made angels in the snow and baked Toad-in-a-Hole. They lay on the carpet listening to CDs. They made love. Alistair never felt so accompanied in his life. It was his first love, he was bursting with happiness, but he couldn't share it with his family. He felt that if he didn't tell somebody about Brian he would die. There was a cousin who lived in America, whom he knew was not close to his parents. She had married a Caucasian, and they disapproved of her. Alistair had her email address, and asked for her telephone number. He called her over Christmas. It was an experiment, his first "coming out of the closet" conversation.

"Wow." she said. "Wow."

He was very nervous.

"Are you sure?" she asked.

He assured her.

"Are you seeing someone?"

He told her about Brian.

"Oh, Alistair. You know, I'm happy for you. Love is hard to find, whatever form it comes in. You have my full support."

Alistair clung to the phone receiver, suddenly wanting very much to cry. "You don't think I'm weird or anything, do you?" he asked, sounding like a small boy.

She said no.

"Why not?" he asked, wishing that she was his mother.

She laughed. "Well, I'm a grad student and a Resident Advisor in a college dormitory of about 500 young men and women. You know how I got this RA job? I had to audition for it, and part of the test was a mock scenario where a student comes up to me and says she is thinking about coming out of the closet. I had to demonstrate that I was able to handle this type of situation, otherwise I'm not fit to be an advisor. They take it seriously over here. We get counselor training. You can say I'm a bit of a veteran. That's why I asked you if you are sure. Some people aren't sure, and it can be a very painful struggle. But you seem to have gone past that. I'm relieved. And you know, it's becoming easier and easier now. You will still have to fight, but you will find more people who understand you than say, ten, twenty years ago."

Alistair could hardly believe that there was a place where people were counseled to handle homosexuals with kid gloves. A place where, perhaps, schoolchildren were sent to revere the naked breasts of the Venus de Milo, and there was no shame. Was this a corrupt society, or an enlightened one? He wanted to laugh. He wanted to know if his cousin had the magic bullet, if she could counsel him on the parental angle, but she didn't.

"Why don't you just take it one day at a time." said Joan. "I would advise against doing it over the phone. They feel powerless, far away. You are in a magic forest. They can't reach you. Their natural instinct would be to drag you out of it at once, to protect you. You might not want that."

⁂

When summer came, Brian moved back to Manchester. Although they had broken up, they raked up huge phone bills calling each other. Alistair worked on his graduation show. His parents were very excited about his graduation and impending return to Singapore. His father said that he had spoken to Yvette's father-in-law, who introduced him to the head surgeon at the National University Hospital, who told him that Alistair could get a residency the instant he came home.

"I've had it all set up, don't worry," said his father. "And by the way, I've invested in a town and country club membership for you. The town club is near your hospital. So you can use it to play tennis at lunch time. On weekends you can go swim and play golf in the country club. It cost me over one hundred *kay*, but I think it's really worth it."

Golf. Alistair wrote in his notebook. *Golf, Folf, Tolf. Golf.*

He was buried in designs for his graduation show. He took up an interest in costume design, and talked to his faculty advisers about getting a gig for a theater or a movie production company. He went to a production of *Romeo and Juliet* by the Royal Shakespeare Company, and wrote a piece in the student newspaper saying that "costumes should not just be a prop expense in a Shakespearean production. *Who is making these god-awful clothes?*" He volunteered to do the costumes for a small theater group which was ambitiously putting up a John Webster play. So he doubled his workload that summer and was smoking himself silly. Hash calmed him.

"I really should stop," he giggled on the phone to Brian, crumbling hash into cigarette paper. "I might become *addicted*." It was not true, of course: Alistair discovered that he could smoke marijuana and tobacco, on and off, without particularly being enslaved by either. But he was on a downward spiral; he liked to think of his habits as addictive. "You know, I know people in Singapore who are addicted to golf. Isn't it funny. I prefer being addicted to hash. It's cheaper. More convenient, too. You can't play golf while watching something on the telly. Or after sex."

"Alistair, you're pissed."

"I just came back from the pub with the lads."

"Are you working on your show? It's next week."

"I am. Maybe." Alistair waived his joint over the piles and piles of paper, the Polaroids on the walls. "I think I have over-committed myself. And the folks back in Singapore are talking about setting me up at the local hospital. Brain surgeon! I'm a fashion designer, for fuck's sake! And you know what? My mum. She's planning a big party to celebrate my graduation. No, no, in *Singapore*. She's not coming *here*. She'll *never* come here. And she says, she is going to introduce me to somebody's daughter, some *stupid cow*, who went to Yvette's secondary school."

"Alistair." Brian raised his voice warily. "You have to tell them the truth."

Alistair screamed. He stamped his feet against the wall. Drawings fluttered to the ground.

"You have to, sooner or later. They must be made to understand."

"It's easy for you to say. You don't have my parents." Alistair ran the back of his hand over his nose. "You know that scene, in *Alice in Wonderland*? The Queen says, 'Sentence first—verdict afterwards!' Off with her head, Brian. Off with her head! And Alice says—"

"Alistair, you're not making sense, you're pissed."

"And Alice says, 'Who cares for *you*? You're nothing but a pack of cards!' And they all explode into a thousand pieces and sh-she wakes up, and it was just a dream. It's brilliant. I wish I could say that to them.'" Alistair dragged the phone across the room and collapsed on the bed, crawling under the bedclothes. His voice sounded muffled. "They have it all set up, the golf club. The job. The arranged marriage. She's the daughter of an engineer. An engineer! Big, fucking, deal. My mum sent them copies of my secondary school exam results, my baby photos. I don't know these people any more. What kind of world they live in. I don't know anymore." Alistair began to cry. "I am so *fucking* unhappy. I am so *fucked up*."

The next day, he woke up with his face all crumpled, and Brian was at the door, wearing his stupid band T-shirt and carrying his battered guitar case.

Alistair's graduation show was a bit of a mixed bag. The top buyers and recruiters failed to attend, and very few students got job offers. But his designs for the theater company caught the attention of the theater community, and he met with several producers who wanted him to design their next show. He postponed his return to Singapore. He read E.M. Forster's *Maurice*. He went to Stratford-upon-Avon to meet with a producer and was hired to make the costumes for *Twelfth Night*. He obtained a work visa after some difficulty. He and Brian moved to Stratford that autumn to work on the production. Brian got a job in the local radio station. They rented a canal boat and paddled up and down the Avon. They saw the sun sink in the horizon behind dark trees and smelled the resinous smoke of wood fires. They watched plays and concerts for free and went to parties in the dim little flats of actors and musicians. Alistair did not tell his parents of his new phone number or his address. He simply said that he had accepted a job in the UK and would let them know once he settled down. He said it in a letter, so that he did not have to listen to savage outbursts on the telephone.

He got an email from Yvette, full of reproach. He read it at the theater. They were rehearsing *Twelfth Night* upstairs. The actors' lines came into his office through a speaker mounted on the wall. He felt cosy and surrounded. Yvette's beam from an alien planet bounced off him. He barely registered words like "disappointed", "party cancelled", and "ingratitude". A few weeks later, an email came from his father, who angrily demanded that Alistair reimburse him for the "seventy-five *kay*" bond that he had posted to the Singapore Government that guaranteed his return in time to serve his National Service. He was tempted to write back ("sell the golf club membership"), but he didn't. When further emails came, he deleted them unopened.

The only person outside of his circle in England that he wrote to was his cousin Joan in Washington, D.C. She often called to see how he was doing, and he emailed her photographs of his production designs, of him and Brian on holiday. The following spring, she sent him pictures of her new baby, a half-white, half-Chinese little girl with rosebud lips. He used a program in his office at the theater to blow up the picture and print it. The baby was tiny, quirky and beautiful. He put her up amid his Polaroids and drawings on the wall.

"Can you believe it, Tom and I haven't come up with a name!" laughed Joan.

His eyes strayed at the last word he had doodled in his notebook.

"Iphigenia."

"What's that, something Greek?"

Alistair explained that it was the name he gave to his first design collection, and it was the name of the daughter Agamemnon planned to sacrifice at Aulis to calm the winds so that his troops could sail to Troy. Even as he said it, he bit his lip; it sounded a bit unlucky, and Joan was, after all, a Chinese mother.

As usual, she surprised him. "You know, that's a bit apt. You guys are the new generation. You have to bear the burden so that more people like you can be accepted back home for who they are. You're paving the way for future kids."

He told her that his first collection had created an uproar at his school and was now legend among the new student generation. *Iphigenia at Aulis*, the collection that chose happiness, despite the bitter springs from which it came.

"Iphigenia never was sacrificed," he said, suddenly, not wanting to omit a happy ending. "At the very last moment the gods switched her for a deer, and then swept her off to faraway lands."

"Iphigenia," Joan pronounced the name over and over again, trying it out. "Yeah, I like it. I like it very much indeed."

DOG HOT POT

THE SUBJECT OF THE Chinese consumption of dog meat attracted my attention when I was just starting out as a research fellow at a university in Wisconsin.

It was a particularly snowy winter. I was alone in my apartment redrafting my thesis proposal for the sixth time. There is nothing more boring in the world than writing a *proposal*—writing about writing a paper. God, kill me now. The old iron radiator was hissing and banging away because I had forgotten to drain it, but I left it that way. I liked the sound.

I was studying food culture and history. It was more difficult to come up with a viable thesis proposal than if I was simply specializing in Kafka or biogenetics. Already nobody in my family back in Singapore took me seriously ("Doesn't sound right for a boy to study this"); sometimes it was a challenge for the faculty to as well. They were threatening to shut down my department: "we cannot keep awarding PhDs on the basis of research on reviving classic strains of tomatoes and aubergines." Not even an impassioned letter from a famous chef in Berkeley (whom I had met during a Paris conference about potatoes) helped convince the university that it was imperative for Americans, in the age of melting polar ice-caps and stem cell research, to continue funding a Chinese Singaporean man's study of the food history of white people.

I was feeling rather depressed and considering making my ninth cup of hot chocolate when Barney, my Golden Retriever mix, barked. I looked at the clock and realized that I hadn't fed Barney since I got up that morning. I went out into the living room and saw him sitting right in front of the television, his huge pink tongue hanging out. He was attracted by the sight of the many dogs on television and lots of people shouting and waving placards. It was a demonstration.

"Move your big butt, Barney," I said, turning up the volume. The news featured the advent of some special annual festival in Korea when dog meat was consumed. Protesters in the United States and in Great Britain had taken to the streets. The footage showed dogs of all colors and sizes, crammed in what looked like chicken coops.

"The dogs are often tortured to death," said the Korean American reporter rather eagerly. "It is believed that the pain suffered by the dog improves its flavor."

Riveting. Barney and I watched the whole thing.

"You're drawing an arbitrary line," said Nancy at the dinner table that evening, when I brought up the topic. "We eat cows and pigs. So some people eat dogs and cats. They're all animals. Don't tell me it's not cruel to take a pig's life."

Nancy was vegetarian; I thought she was going to support me. It is a sad truism that in marriage one expects a complete harmony of minds. The slightest disagreement jars, irritates, and then begins to assume gargantuan proportions. In this case, I was beginning to doubt Nancy's morals. Where were her *values*?

"I cannot believe it," I whistled, feeling a slight unpleasant tingle at the base of my neck, which often preceded one of our rare arguments. "You're a vegetarian and you don't think eating dogs is wrong?"

"You're just being arbitrary." repeated Nancy.

I looked at Barney, who looked back.

I tried a different tact.

"Well, what about the fact that I feel *uncomfortable* as a Chinese person that there is this reported tendency of East Asians to consume animals that have been adopted by other cultures as pets? I mean, does the interdependence between man and dog, the relationships passed down for thousands of years between man and the animals he had

17

chosen to domesticate, count for *nothing*?" I gestured. "We're not talk-ing about cows. Nobody keeps cows as pets."

Nancy stared at me. I remembered her curious cousin in upstate New York.

"Well, almost nobody," I said hastily. "But dogs and cats are widely kept companion animals. You can't have half the planet adoring them and the other half eating them. Anyway, most people around the world eat the same few animals—cow, chicken—why do Asians have to set themselves apart with this dog thing? Why hasn't the practice died out? I mean, drowning of girl babies has died out, hasn't it?"

Nancy was getting that glazed look in her eyes—the look you give to an academic for whom every dinner conversation is "discourse" and "dialectic." She said there was nothing in it, that I needn't try to ferret out some theory about Asians. I couldn't help it. I had been for too many years in a generous American academic environment where stu-dents were given infinite time and resources to pry apart the most banal facts of life and put it under a microscope. I got a scholarship for studying the history of corn. It was still a constant source of amuse-ment for my Singaporean friends and relatives.

I said, "You know how people joke about how the Chinese would eat anything on four legs, except tables and chairs?"

"Why get so upset over the Chinese angle?" retorted Nancy. "I'm sure my ancestors in Ireland consumed rats during the potato famine. It doesn't mean I would personally consume rats. You're always getting so upset when some Asian person in the world does something that you wouldn't do. You always think it reflects badly on you. You're not even Korean."

"The Chinese also eat dogs. And cats," I said hotly. I leaned across the dinner table, forgetting about the meal, and said earnestly, ticking off my fingers, "And turtles. Turtle cartilage, to be exact; they boil it down into jelly. And bear's paws, and tiger's penises, and crocodiles, and antelope horn. It doesn't bother you?"

"So? The Maoris used to eat human beings. They thought little boy's fingers were a delicacy."

Anyone who had popped their head into our kitchen at that moment would have thought we were a rather odd couple. Nancy was Irish American and grew up in Oregon; I grew up in Singapore. Nancy had what I liked to call a quintessential American trait: an unrelentingly broad view of the world. Nothing shocked her. Something which would keep a Singaporean awake at night—don't ask me what, there were a lot of things—Nancy would not only be untroubled by, but instantly rationalize and find some justification for it. In my more generous moods, I often think: *here is a white woman whose ancestors went forth stubbornly as missionaries in the malarial jungles of Africa and Asia.* The kind of people who would be the last to leave during a civil war, protecting babies and orphans.

"Nancy, all I am asking is, why do the Chinese eat dogs? Do my people in Singapore eat dogs?"

"If you're starving you would eat anything."

"Yes, but it's not just the starving who eat dogs. There has got to be something deeper than that. And anyway, how could you be so blasé about this? Can't you just stop being so rational for God's sake and give me a gut reaction, as a dog owner? Would you let them eat Barney?" I pleaded, pointing to the dog we had rescued from the pound six years ago.

"That's a totally different issue," said Nancy diplomatically, clearing away the tofu salad and vegetarian lasagna. "Look, if it bothers you so much, why don't you write your thesis about it."

Thus began a series of rather odd meals I had in the Far East.

❦

I hadn't been back to Singapore for many years, so it was with some trepidation that I approached my home country to discern their eating habits.

It was raining heavily the day I went to visit a Malay journalist friend of mine. We had been classmates in primary school. He came down his apartment block to greet me at the taxi stand, holding a pink

19

toy umbrella that said *Power Puff Girls* in purple balloon font.

"Don't know where my wife keeps the umbrellas," said Ibrahim as we walked to his block. "Just grabbed my daughter's. Anyway, with this type of rain, you know any kind of umbrella isn't going to be of any bloody use."

He was absolutely right, of course. I was unprepared for tropical rain and foolishly forgot an umbrella. It turned out that there were a lot of things in my own country that I had forgotten. The heat, the humidity, the fact that taxi drivers give change. When we got to Ibrahim's flat, I cut straight to the chase and asked him what he thought about the Chinese eating dogs.

"I tell you what's gross that Chinese people eat," said Ibrahim, his eyes twinkling. "*Babi.* Pig."

"*Aiyoh*, Ibrahim, why suddenly talk about pig," his wife Farah tut-tutted, bringing out another tray of trim little green cakes.

"See, it's like poison, we can't even discuss babi in the house," laughed Ibrahim. "It's a pathological fear. Ask my little daughter. Nadia, come here."

His eight-year-old dropped her pencil and came over shyly.

"Tell Uncle Christopher about pigs."

"My least favorite animal," announced Nadia. "*Babi*, yuck."

"You don't even like to look at them?" I asked.

Her mother looked rather exasperated and explained. "When she was little I told her we are Muslim so we have to be careful about accidentally eating pork products, but it turned out that she started avoiding pigs like crazy. If she was reading a book and there was a pig in it, she would throw the book clean across the room. If she was coloring a coloring book, she would color all the animals except the pig. She cried when my Chinese friend took her to see Babe the movie with the other kids. So embarrassing! Once, we took her to the Night Safari, and the kids were all scared of the lion and the panther, and Nadia just ran off screaming when this little wild pig trotted up the path to her. You should have seen her."

Later on, when her parents were in the kitchen, little Nadia came over to me and whispered in my ear, "My grandmother says, Chinese people smell like pig."

I feigned astonishment. "What about me? Do I smell like pig?"

She sniffed. "Don't know. Are you Chinese? You live in America."

"Yes, I'm Chinese. I'm from Singapore just like you."

"Mummy says you're American. So how can you be Chinese and Singaporean and American at the same time?"

I got that a lot, and not just from eight-year-olds.

"Tell me, what do you think if I told you Chinese people ate dogs?" I sure wasn't doing my race a favor, but it was worth a try. My thesis did not have a lower age limit on survey respondents.

Her eyes widened and she pretended to look terrified. She raised her fingers above her head and made a creepy leer. Then she dissolved into hysterical giggles.

"Dogs? Like 101 *Dalmatians*?"

"Yes."

Then she pouted. "You're bluffing."

Her parents called us in for dinner. Fried fish, prawn *sambal*, and beef *rendang*.

I went to visit Peter Tang, a friend of mine who was a veterinarian. He was one of the few people in Singapore I knew who carried photographs of his cats in his wallet (a habit he acquired when studying in the United Kingdom). We instantly started exchanging stories of our pets, as if they were our children. His cat, Happy, was suffering from kidney failure. Any day now, Peter said, his eyes tearing up. I told him about Barney's rheumatic hip, and we discussed the kinds of treatments for retrievers in the United States and compared them with what was available in Singapore.

"We don't have that kind of treatment here," sighed Peter. "You can get more types of things in the U.S."

"Yeah, I notice everybody in Singapore keeps saying that. I can get more types of books, clothes, handbags, DVD's, you name it. It's like the whole nation is constantly pining away for consumer goods in America," I said. "Why don't you think about what you can't get in America?"

"Like what?"

"Like *roti prata*."

Peter protested, "Rubbish, you can get that in America now. You can get that in London."

"Yeah, *roti prata* doesn't taste good unless you eat it in the surly morning tropical heat in a noisy coffee shop and while you're eating you see the Indian cook making the next one right in front of you."

Peter, like most Singaporeans, preferred the Martyr's Mantle of Chronic Deprivation. He gave me this look that suggested that he would prefer to have easy access to 300 cable channels any day than the privilege of consuming an Indian fried pancake at a corner stand.

Then I told him about the student demonstrations in the United States. I was confident that he would be on my side, that we were soaked in the same values. After all, he was an animal lover.

"You are always trying to prove that there is something wrong with us Chinese," laughed Peter. We went to a coffee bar and waited for his wife to join us for lunch. "I can tell you Singaporean Chinese don't eat dogs and cats anymore. Go out into the street and ask anyone. They'll think you're mad."

I confessed that as a Singaporean Chinese person who had lived abroad for a long time, I had evolved into a sort of self-appointed Public Relations Officer for the entire Chinese race. Yes, all one billion of them.

"You have no idea," I said. "In America, every time a white person sees some news report about Asians eating dogs, they look at me funny, because I have a dog. I swear to God we have this neighbor who gave me dirty looks after PETA organized a protest on our campus about dog meat consumption during the World Cup thing in Korea. When we first adopted Barney from the pound, the staff asked Nancy some really strange questions, just to make sure I wasn't just getting a free puppy for the pot."

"So?" said Peter nonchalantly. "Say you're Singaporean Chinese, not someone from mainland China."

"Are you nuts? *They* don't know the difference."

"Tell them it's obvious Singaporeans don't eat dogs. We're too busy queuing up for *bak kwa* from Lim Chee Guan." Peter cracked up at his own joke.

I explained that I was doing my thesis on this issue and was just trying to gauge cultural reactions, starting with my home town. Peter dug a crumpled brochure out of his pocket and handed it over.

"I found this in my office from some animal rights people and thought you might want it."

List of countries where dog and cat meat consumption has been reported: ANGOLA, ARGENTINA, CAMBODIA, CAMEROON, CANADA, CHINA ,CUBA, EGYPT (ANCIENT), GHANA, HONG KONG, JAPAN, LAGOS, MEXICO, NIGERIA, PHILIPPINES, SOVIET UNION (NEAR ASIA), SWITZERLAND (HISTORICAL), TAIWAN, THAILAND, UNITED STATES, VIETNAM.

"See?" said Peter emphatically. "It's not just the Chinese."

"Wait. It says here that in the Asian countries, most of the dog-eating *today* is perpetrated by Chinese immigrants. Same for dog-eating in the U.S. and Canada."

Peter's face fell.

"See?" I retorted. "There's something about us, Peter. I have to get to the bottom of it. I have to find out what Singaporeans think about dog-eating."

Just then, a rather pregnant lady waved at us.

"Surprise!" said Linda, patting her abdomen. "Number two!"

I congratulated them. I remembered how I was inundated with JPEG photographs of their son when he was born a few years before.

"What a big *hoo-ha* that was," I smiled. "The most expensive hospital, the best pediatrician."

"Oh, no, no more of that," said Peter hastily.

Linda took his arm and smiled confidently. "Yah, it's only a girl this time. No need to spend so much money."

๛

"Well, I can tell you one thing," said my great-aunt Madam Pang pointedly. I was having dim sum with her in a bustling Cantonese restaurant. "You will find that Chinese Buddhists condemn the practice. Just the other day, I was at the temple chatting with some of the elderly ladies, when someone brought up the topic of dog hot pot. She had just gone to visit her son who was working for some oil company in Beijing, and it was winter. And everywhere, they were selling dog hot pot. Signs in the windows, *gou huo guo*." She trailed off, suddenly. "Hmm, kind of strange, isn't it. Dog hot pot, *gou huo guo*, the phrase is rather hard to say, both in English and Mandarin. Like a tongue twister. Sticks in your throat."

I exclaimed that that was exactly how repugnant I found the concept. She smiled rather indulgently.

"Well, anyway, this lady said she was so shocked because she never knew that Chinese people ate dog, and ate it so casually, too. We had some discussion about whether they actually farmed the same species of dog for consumption, or just got stray dogs off the street, in which case, you never know what species you are eating, would you? So how would you be assured of the flavor? Wouldn't you get a completely different dish each time, depending on the breed? That's what she asked her son, who said that to make the dog meat taste good, they beat and torture the dogs. Something about the adrenalin making the meat tender."

She shuddered.

"So scary, isn't it? And then the ladies at the Buddhist temple all declared that they would never eat dog, and you know why?" My great aunt lowered her soup spoon and raised her tattooed eyebrows dramatically. Her voice sank to a conspiratorial whisper. "*Because the dog could be the reincarnation of a human being.*"

I wrote it all down.

๛

"So? Have you found any Singaporeans who have eaten dog hot pot?"

My wife's voice came over the telephone with the trace of a faint echo. I heard Barney barking. She said, "I've trained him to bark in protest every time I say *dog hot pot*. Here, listen to this. Dog hot pot. (Bark). Dog hot pot (Bark). He knows what it means, the smart lad. Here, talk to him."

I had encamped in my old room at my parents' house, a five-room HDB flat in a very old part of town. It smelled of mould, mothballs, and old mattresses. It was a familiar smell. I was about to say something to Nancy when the door to my bedroom rattled and then jerked open suddenly. It was my mother, who had never learned to knock before entry. It didn't matter now that I was over thirty, but it used to bother me. A lot.

"Do you mind?" I covered the phone receiver. "I'm talking to Barney."

"Who's Barney?" asked my mother. Except she said "Barley", because she was Teochew and always had difficulty with "n" names. Nancy was *Lancy*, and so on.

"Barley is my dog."

She threw up her hands and said, "Your father has come home and dinner is ready." She left the room, shaking her head, muttering to herself, *when is he going to get a real career and make money.*

I hung up on Nancy shortly and went out to the dim little dining room (the special one that they only used for "guests"—most of the time my parents ate in the kitchen). Although it was not the best topic to be brought out at meal time, over dinner I tried to explain to my parents my thesis research.

"It's only the Koreans," grunted my father. "Those people eat everything. The Chinese are more high-class."

"Actually, the Koreans claim that the practice came from the Chinese, several thousand years back." I pointed out. "And they still serve dog hot pot in China these days."

Cornered, my father changed the subject. "So, when are you coming home?"

"Dad, do we have to discuss this right now? It's such an open-ended question."

There he was, the old pater, chopsticks in his right hand, rice bowl in his other. I was thirteen again.

"Your cousins tell me you are studying all kinds of nonsense. Corn! You study corn! How can you make money? When are you going to come home and start a family? We bought you this flat nearby and you never come back to stay in it. For years we have been renting it out at a loss. Hoping our son will come home to his country. You know, just the other day our MPs were complaining again about brain drain."

I delighted in the assonance, but he probably didn't notice.

"He said, we feed you and house you, give you vaccinations, Toothbrushing Campaign, School Milk Program, free public education. And then you go and give your talents to some other country," grunted my father.

I said that he was perfectly right; I had a great set of teeth that never needed any work, which remained a marvel to my university dentists. They told me that they were used to seeing foreign students with awful teeth and never failed to ask me where I was from.

"When I told them about our primary school Toothbrushing Campaign at recess, my dentist thought she was in heaven." I said jovially.

"Then why are you not coming back?" demanded my father.

"Dad, good teeth is not a reason to remain in one's country."

My father snapped, "What more do you want?" He was losing his temper, and my mother interceded anxiously, mumbling something about whether we wanted to try her red bean dessert.

"You remember I am married now." I reminded him mildly. "Everything would have to be a joint decision." Oops, red rag to a bull.

My father drew his eyebrows together imperiously. "Who told you to marry a foreigner? You make your own life so complicated. Anyway, she can come work here. They always need expat teachers."

I told him that Nancy was a physiotherapist, not an English language teacher, but the fact slid off like a drop of water on a duck's back.

"I have told you before and I will tell you again, you are only

26

asking for trouble by marrying a Caucasian. You know those Americans don't have the concept of marriage. They have a fifty per cent divorce rate. She's not going to be faithful to you. I have never heard of a Chinese man marrying an *ang moh* where it ended well."

My mother said something about there being some famous Asian politicians who have married white women and that it did not seem to interfere too much with their political careers. The old man looked at her, ignored the adduced evidence, and simply said "it" (whatever "it" was) was "all her fault".

Over the years I had mastered the art of sidestepping my father's prejudices. I had come here to find out why Asians eat dog meat, not to listen to another round of the usual anti-American gunfire. I simply remarked, as I sipped red bean soup, that I did not return to Singapore because I would not have been able to get a scholarship in my home country to study the history and political implications of the corn trade.

"I just don't understand," sighed my mother weakly, "how you can go overseas to study this kind of thing. Other people study law, medicine, maybe computer science. I'm always so embarrassed when people ask me what you're studying."

"It's a joke, that's what it is!" roared my father. "He got 12 A1's in his 'O' Levels and he wastes it on studying *jiagong*! I don't know what kind of university encourages this type of studies."

The fact that I wrote a paper on corn irritated him no end, particularly because the word for "corn" sounded like the Chinese word for "stupid" or "retard". It was perhaps why my father loves to call Americans "stupid, slow-witted corn-fed folk". Wait a minute. Yes, this could be worth pursuing. Did corn make you stupid? I made a mental note to discuss this over with my professor, whose specialty was racism and dietary regimes. My father was still fulminating, but already I was mentally writing a chapter of my thesis.

※

27

"I tell you why the Singaporean Chinese don't eat dogs," said Ibrahim, as we drove to the airport. "They're too damned sentimental. They like Hello Kitty. Have you ever passed by the Sanrio store at lunch hour? All the office girls packing the store, buying Hello Kitty. I bet none of them eat dogs."

"Well, whatever it is, I'm glad that in Singapore I have unearthed evidence of eating—" I flipped open one of my notebooks and continued, "—bats, snakes, frogs, fish ovaries, chicken cartilage, turtles, duck fetuses, antelope horn, crocodile meat, crickets (dried)—but no dogs and cats."

"That's all, huh," said Ibrahim. "I thought you Chinese ate all kinds of things. Monkey's brains? Bear's paws? Unicorns? You know what they say: the Chinese eat everything on four legs except tables and chairs!"

"Well, based on my survey, they may love their pets but still think girl babies are inferior; they think white people are stupid and lazy; and that people should marry within their own race; and that all a man ever wants to do is to be a lawyer or doctor and make money and live in a big house. But at least my people here have dropped the dog habit from old Mother China." I grinned as he drew up at the curb and we unloaded my baggage. "It's progress."

"Hey, take it one day at a time," said Ibrahim, winking, and shook my hand.

THE MAN WHO WAS AFRAID
OF ATMS

C HANG WAITED FOR HIS granddaughter in the hot stillness of the car. He was parked outside the gates of Fairleigh Girls' School, which, according to his son, was the most expensive private school in Ontario. Certainly the students seemed to have expensive uniforms. Navy blue woolen blazers and tartan kilts for the winter. Crisp white blouses and pert tennis skirts for the summer. Chang disapproved. Too dressy, he had said, when Sylvie first paraded around in her different uniforms at home.

The child was delighted. It was a hint of things to come, she said. Already she noted that the Canadian school uniforms were of higher quality, made from pure wool and cotton, nothing like the scratchy, polyester-mix affairs she had to wear in Singapore. They made you feel glamorous, rather than dumbed you down. All her schoolmates in Singapore were jealous and refused to talk to her by the time she left. She was going to spend Christmas where there was snow. And perhaps, Sylvie said, there would be old manor houses with smoking chimneys. And horses with horse traps. After all, Ontario was near Prince Edward Island, said the ten-year-old Sylvie at recess to her schoolmates, opening her pocket atlas. That was where Anne of Green Gables lived. Her friends were all fans of Anne of Green Gables. The world of Edwardian Canada made their tight little rosebud souls open. They yearned for long skirts, balls, and sandy-haired boys with freckles and straw boaters. They couldn't believe that one among them was lucky enough to enter the ranks of the Elect, to merge into the misty havens of the West and leave prefects, G.C.E. 'O' Levels, and the sweltering tropical heat behind. Their ice-cream lollies dripped enviously into the gutter as they crouched at the end of the basketball court, looking at Sylvie's atlas, watching her fingers trace across unknown towns, craggy coastlines and imagining the cool foam of perilous seas, in fairy lands forlorn, until the school bell rang.

"You look like a Western girl," said Chang of her uniform on her first day at Fairleigh.

"I feel like something out of a Harry Potter book!" said Sylvie, admiring her school scarf.

Chang had never read Harry Potter. Never heard of him. For over forty-five years, he had worked as a Chinese language teacher in secondary schools in Singapore. Like his scholar father, he had a Chinese education, which got him into some trouble with the Singapore authorities during the Communist riots in the sixties. In his study in Singapore he collected hundreds of volumes of books published in Taiwan and Hong Kong. Later, in the eighties, he started getting books from China again. Most of his books were printed on thin, see-through rice paper, filled with tiny, furious little strings of characters marching resolutely from top to bottom, from right to left. They used to amuse Sylvie's father, Leng, when he was little. Like Sylvie, Leng grew up with an English language education. When Leng got married, he converted to Christianity so that the wedding could be held in a beautiful church. There being only two large Chinese tribes in Singapore—those who received their education in English, and those who went to traditional Chinese schools—Chang soon found himself across a great divide from his only son. Perhaps that was why Leng got mad at him when he wanted to move his books when they emigrated together.

"They'll take up a whole entire container, " said Leng. "Are these old books really worth the shipping costs?"

There were love stories, stories of political betrayal, stories of warriors and clever judges and corrupt magistrates and witty courtesans. And whole boxed sets of *wuxia xiaoshuo*, Chinese martial arts epics which he loved and memorized by heart, long before they became popularized and adapted by Hong Kong television dramas. In his school days he used to write *wuxia xiaoshuo*, and even had minor publishing success in the evening newspapers' literary sections. Then, one by one, the Chinese newspapers shut down in Singapore. Leng read Enid Blyton and Hardy Boys. By the time Sylvie came along, it was Anne of Green Gables and Harry Potter.

"Grandpa, your books are funny-looking," Sylvie would say. A lover of books herself, she often came into his study and fingered his volumes. "They don't have pictures on the covers. How would you know what they are about?" She sniffed. "They smell funny." The dry, papery smell of Chinese press books and Chinese inks, which reminded him so much more of trees and leaves and dead things. The pages yellowed in a season and the blue-gray print smudged if you rubbed your finger too hard against it. The thin paper covers tore easily. Like the blocky, bitty ideograms they contained, the books themselves felt ancient, like stacks of hieroglyphed papyruses entombed in the sagging teak bookshelves of Chang's study. Sylvie preferred her brand new English paperbacks, each designed and launched at the pre-teen market with the resources of multi-million dollar Anglo-American publishing empires. They stood on the shelves of bookstores, glittering like brightly-wrapped bars of chocolate. Her parents lavished them on her.

"Your own grandfather is a Chinese teacher, and yet you do not read Chinese books," he used to chide her gently.

"But there are no books written for young people in Chinese," said Sylvie.

"You could read stories of the Monkey King. Children enjoy that."

"But I want stories written about people *like me*."

"But you're not like the children in the English books you read," said Chang. "You're a Chinese girl."

Sylvie looked confused. As her grandfather smiled, she lost her temper and stomped out of the room.

꙰

Another time, she announced, "When I grow up I'm going to study literature at university."

31

"English literature or Chinese literature?" asked Chang.

"English of course," said Sylvie. She tried to hide it, but he caught her contempt. He recognized it in his students as well. The fifties and sixties taught much of the world that being Chinese was backward. It was a burden that could be at times hard to bear.

Once, Sylvie came into his room and asked, "Is there such a thing as Chinese literature?"

"Yes, of course. What do you think this is?" He pointed to his collection.

"Do you have any with English translations, then?" she asked hopefully.

He laughed. "You know, Sylvie, Chinese literature pre-dates English literature by many thousands of years."

"That's not true!" She was shocked, her eyes widened.

"Ask your daddy and mummy."

"Older than Shakespeare?"

"Yes."

"Older than the *Bible*?"

"Possibly."

"You know, my Chinese teacher said at school that there are more Chinese people in the world than English people."

"That could be true."

"That's impossible. *Everyone* speaks English now! *Everywhere*."

Chang laughed to himself as he recollected her insistence. He did not argue with her. He looked at his watch and wondered where she was. The flood of Fairleigh schoolgirls had thinned out. He had the opportunity to study them individually and once again remembered that he was no longer in Asia. The students at Sylvie's school were mostly white. They were big, strong, beefy, he thought, still acclimatizing to Caucasian youth after a lifetime of teaching Asian kids. The Fairleigh girls looked, as his late wife would have said, "so matured." They wore makeup and styled their hair into thick, glossy ponytails. They burgeoned out of their white blouses and skirts like female Goliaths. Occasionally, an Asian girl scattered in their midst would twinkle out, a gazelle among elephants.

He distrusted white girls. They talked too loudly and moved too fast, and when they laughed, they showed their broad pink tongues. They pierced their ears with multiple studs. He was glad he didn't have to teach them. They looked like the type who would answer back, and they rose half a head taller than him. Chang shuddered to think what the boys' school would be like. He remembered his students in Singapore. The boys, bungling in adolescence, laughing their nervous laughs. During their breaks, they fought imaginary wars with wooden rulers. The girls, with their blue-black hair and pink pencil boxes, who cried easily when they did badly on a test. They grew up into skinny girls who worked in offices in Shenton Way and clickety-clacked their way across marble floors in their Ferragamo pumps. They would recognize and greet him as "Teacher" still, in public places, even though many years had passed. He was glad they grew up into proper women. Compared to them, the peachy, rotund fecundity of the girls at Sylvie's school was alarming. They seem to tear through life quickly with a kind of wasteful abandon.

The other day, he was alone at home flicking through cable channels when he caught a Nike advertisement showing a young woman emerging from a Wall Street office. She stripped off her black pantsuit, changed, and then proceeded to run down a long, leafy road in her Nike gear. She was tall and her blond ponytail bounced along as she coasted with the wind in determination. She was a picture of athletic strength, an urban Athena. Chang thought suddenly, *this is what Sylvie's going to grow up into*. He panicked. She seemed to be running away from him, hurtling towards a kind of mechanized, modernized, Americanized future that had no place for people like him. The thought of a world where a woman could go running for hours alone, just for the sheer hell of it, made him uncomfortable.

An angry buzzing interrupted his thoughts. He looked around in the car confusedly, then realized it was the mobile phone that Leng had bought for him.

"Dad, where are you?" It was Sylvie's mother.

"Picking Sylvie up."

"Have you forgotten? It's Tuesday. On Tuesdays she's got drama class so she won't be out till half past seven."

Chang started. "Oh! Oh I see. No, I forgot. Ha ha. I'm old. Why is she taking drama class?"

His daughter-in-law sounded exasperated. "That's what Fairleigh is famous for, their theater program. They've sent girls to Juilliard, to RADA."

Sounded like types of medicine, he thought. He pretended to get it. Annette was very chic, and for Leng's sake he always "got" what she was saying. He knew her opinion of his English, since he was a Chinese teacher, so he was always on his guard. For her sake, he learned to pronounce "prosciutto," he looked up the word "pergola".

"Anyway, will you be home by five o'clock, because I'm actually expecting a delivery?"

"Sure, sure." Chang thought he sounded too eager to please. When he was younger, fathers-in-law were to be feared. They were patriarchs; they had certain privileges and entitlements. But here he was, in a strange country with his only son and daughter-in-law, and by their grace he intended to live out the rest of his years. He was a chauffeur, a butler, to his daughter-in-law with her black turtlenecks and her six figure investment banker salary. If his wife were alive, she would have thought he was doing the right thing. After all, he was retired. What else were old people good for?

Annette left instructions for him for the delivery guy. Five hundred dollars cash, and get a receipt. It was a *cheongsam* that was tailor-made for her to be worn to a benefit that night, and "very important". If they didn't deliver it by five o'clock, he was to call her right away. He offered to pick it up instead, but she reminded him that he didn't know downtown Toronto very well and was likely to lose his way. She was perfectly right. If the store wasn't in Chinatown, he would have no idea how to get there.

"Thanks, Dad. And don't worry about Sylvie, Mrs Crenshaw will drop her off at home this evening."

He started up the engine and pulled slowly out of the sun-drenched lot. He was still nervous about driving in Canada. It was true that he had driven for nearly fifty years in Singapore, but he failed his driving test over and over again in Canada. It led to a crisis of confidence from which he never recovered. Once, he was flagged down by Canadian highway patrol when he was picking up Sylvie.

"Not to worry," Chang said cheerfully to his granddaughter, who was utterly absorbed in the latest Harry Potter book in the backseat. She seemed not to have noticed anything.

He watched with a sick feeling in his guts as the burly cop stepped out of his car. Why are foreign cops always so burly? he thought to himself. Physical bulk did not seem a prerequisite for the law enforcement profession in Singapore. The cop's face was inscrutable under reflective aviator sunglasses. He strode up slowly, looking at the back of the car.

"Sylvie, Sylvie," croaked Chang, his throat dry. "Hey, girl. Sylvie!"

"What?"

"Can you talk to the policeman for me?"

"No," said Sylvie, flipping a page. Harry Potter was going to win the wizard triathlon, or was he? Her eyes raced effortlessly over the words. So different, he noted, from when she had to read Chinese characters.

"Sylvie, please, the policeman is going to book me! You have to talk to him!"

"Why? What have you done?" Sylvie looked up.

"I don't know what I've done!" he was shouting now. "Y-you talk to him OK! Your English is better!"

The cop tapped at his window and he lowered the glass reluctantly. Chang found that he could not say anything, so he stared straight at the steering wheel, his hands still on it. He was almost furious; his face was red hot with shame. He had never, never been pulled over by a cop, never got a ticket in five decades. He had always been so careful. But he wasn't on his home turf anymore, and who knows, maybe they just like to pick on Chinese people here. Luckily he had Sylvie with him.

"How are you folks doing?" said the cop cheerily.

Chang's scalp pricked. He wasn't going very fast. Maybe he had failed to read a road sign. It wasn't fair.

"Sir? Do you understand English?" asked the cop, lowering his head to peer into the car when Chang failed to respond. Chang nodded. "Just wanted to let you know that your passenger door isn't shut properly, OK? There was a car right behind you who was honking to get your attention about it. Miss, do you mind opening it and shutting it again for me? That's it. Good. Have a good day, folks."

And then, the cop strolled back to his car and drove off. Just like that.

"What a nice guy," said Sylvie cheerfully, arranging herself back in her seat. "I *love* Canadian cops. They're *so cool*."

Chang was transfixed in his seat. Blindly, he pushed the gear back into drive and inched back on the highway. It was not until the wheels of the car crunched into his son's driveway that his stomach began to unclench. Sylvie didn't even mention the incident to her parents.

❧

Every weekday Chang drove the same route from his son's house to Fairleigh Girls', with few variations. He had been in Toronto for almost two years, but his awareness of his geographic surroundings was limited to a few dozen city blocks. He knew how to drive to the school, and to the Sunset Strip Mall, where Annette bought him his winter clothes, and where Sylvie went to watch movies with her friends whenever she was allowed. He knew how to drive to Park Place, where they went to see their doctor and dentist whenever the occasion arose. He knew how to drive to Chinatown and back. Once he knew these few places, he never wanted to go anywhere else. Leng and Annette worked downtown somewhere high up behind smoked glass windows; he didn't even know the names of their companies.

He felt happy in Chinatown. It was the first place he went to by himself when he arrived. Often he would drive himself there and buy

36

roast pork or a whole roast duck, packed in a styrofoam box, for his dinner. He never knew how to cook, but when his wife died and he had to move in with Leng and Annette, he realized that they ate Western. He came to rely on rice boxes from Chinatown. Leng and Annette didn't like to go to Chinatown with him. "Smelly and porky," said Annette. "Dad, I can show you better restaurants downtown," said Leng. "You never want to come out with us."

Annette once asked him why he liked Toronto's Chinatown. "You never seemed to go to the Chinatown in Singapore," she said curiously.

He explained that it was different being in a foreign place. He felt more comfortable being surrounded by Chinese faces, buying from Chinese stores. "At least you know they are not ripping you off," he said.

Annette laughed. "Oh, be careful, Chinese people rip each other off too! And you're not even Cantonese, do you understand what they are saying?"

It was true. Chang had language problems in Chinatown. Mandarin was not widely spoken in the mostly-Cantonese immigrant community in Toronto, and his dialect group was not well-represented. Sometimes a waiter would be rude to him because he didn't know how to ask for something in Cantonese. A spoon was *tang chi* in Mandarin; but *qi gang* in Cantonese. A plastic bag: *su jiao dai* in one language, *kao doi* in another. It was difficult to learn. Those were the times when Chang blamed his Singaporean upbringing. "Our English is not good enough for the English, and our Chinese is not good enough for the Chinese," he said to Leng.

To which Leng replied, "Well, just go eat in the Singapore-Malaysian restaurants, then!"

"They don't cook it right," he grumbled. "And the waiters are still Cantonese." No matter how he tried to fit into Chinatown, he wriggled uncomfortably in his linguistic apparel. It was no better back in his son's neighborhood. Leng chose to buy a house in a mostly-Chinese housing development, built just a year ago by a Hong Kong property developer. Most of his neighbors were either from Hong Kong or

Taiwan. Singapore was too small to be represented.

"Who wants to live next door to a Singaporean anyway!" complained Annette when he mentioned the fact. "Might as well go back to Singapore!"

According to a wildlife documentary Chang saw on cable, chameleons hated company. If another chameleon came near, they would fight and one would be forcibly ejected from the other's territory. Annette reminded him of a chameleon. Once she adapted to fit into her surroundings, she preferred not to be near her own kind.

He remembered suddenly that he was supposed to have five hundred dollars to pay for Annette's *cheongsam*, and that he had meant to get it from the bank. He drove past Sunset Strip Mall and rounded the corner, past the municipal park and its giant parking lot, past Tim Horton's Doughnuts (he never considered it as a culinary possibility), to the little bank with a green roof sitting in its own parking lot. He looked at his watch and realized that it was fast approaching five o'clock. He parked the car and hurried into the bank, then clucked his tongue in exasperation. The bank was filled with last-minute customers anxious to settle the day's transactions.

"Can I help you, sir?" asked the receptionist.

He smiled at her uneasily and looked again at the line. He looked at his watch. He wanted to ask the receptionist if there was an express counter for him to withdraw money, but all that came out were simply the monosyllabic words, "Um. Take out. Cash."

"You'd like to withdraw cash?"

He nodded, blushing. Whenever he had to deal with white people, he found himself blushing and nervous. That never happened in Singapore when he spoke to the occasional white tourist. But here he felt like their guest, navigating among their strange ways.

The receptionist did not seem to have noticed his discomfort. "If you have your ATM card, you can use the machines right outside the door, the line's much shorter outside." She pointed.

He trotted out again, sweating. It was really hot in the bank. He stood in the line for the ATM. She was right, of course, there were only a few people in line, but he was starting to get really furious. He always withdrew money from the counter, with a real person. It was all Annette's fault. Her stupid dress. All this for her silly dress. Why was it so important? An indignation filled him; he trembled. He never liked Annette. Why did his son choose to marry this woman? It was all her fault. He looked behind him, hoping no one would stand in line after him.

Unfortunately, a man and a woman joined the line. They were both white. He kept turning around to look at them, feeling ill.

There were only three people ahead of him, then there were two, then one. It was his turn. He stared at the screen. His eyes blurred. *This is not even in English!* he thought frantically. *I can't read it! I can't read it!* He realized he was staring at the French greeting, in blue, and that the English greeting was above it, in red. His vision swam. Blindly, he keyed in his pin code. He knew his pin code because it was the same one as the one he had used all his life for his ATM card in Singapore. But over here it was all different. This was a foreign ATM machine. And the white people standing behind him were sighing and looking impatient. All for Annette's stupid *cheongsam!* He looked at the screen. Why wasn't it responding? He had already keyed in his pin code. He waited, then the message came up. Did he want to cancel the transaction? He jabbed frantically, No. No. He realized he had forgotten to press "Enter" after entering his pin code. He entered it again, palms moist. *Enter.* The selection came up, did he want to withdraw from his checking or savings account?

He stared, stupefied, at the screen. The display showed arrows pointing to buttons for selection. But the arrows on the screen didn't line up with the actual buttons on the machine, and he couldn't tell which button was for which selection. He guessed, and the machine made an angry buzz. Invalid, please try again.

He heard the man behind sighing impatiently. From the corner of his eye, Chang saw the man turn and say to the woman behind him, "God, don't you love these people?"

Hot tears came to Chang's eyes. He felt sallow and shriveled. At five feet four, he was not even as tall as their children. And he was wearing this ugly brown woolen vest that his late wife had knitted, instead of the nice navy blue blazer with brass buttons that Annette had given him for his birthday. "When we are over here we always have to dress more formally than we did back in Singapore, just in case they think we are fresh off the boat!" she had said. For fifty years he had been a teacher of the most intricate and regal language that the world has known, and they thought he didn't understand the English they were speaking. This would never have happened in Singapore! In Singapore, you knew who you were, and people knew who you were. Within the races there were class markers. Here the infinitesimal differences, so important back home, shrank into nothingness. In the vast landscape of Canada nobody had time to take a closer look at what type of Chinese you were. You tumbled headlong into the same racial trench as the other immigrants with yellow skin. You could be a textile worker, a dim sum waiter, an illegal immigrant; a poet, a painter, a judge. It didn't matter. You were one of "these people", thought Chang. He used to say "these people" when he was in Singapore. He used the phrase to refer to the Indian immigrant workers who lined the streets of Little India on weekends; the Filipina maids crowding the front of a shopping mall in Orchard Road. "These people are really too much," he used to say, whenever he drove past them. "So noisy." And now, someone was referring to him in that tone. It was horribly unfair. Don't they know he wasn't *that* kind of person?

The cash whirred out, he grabbed it and tried to make a dignified exit.

"Hey mister, you forgot your card," said the man loudly.

Chang stumbled back and retrieved his card. It was sticking out like a white tongue from the machine. He did not see the man's face, he did not see the expressions of the other people who had joined the line. He walked quickly down the path back to the car and shut himself in. He was shaking from head to toe, the cash still tightly gripped in his left hand.

The delivery boy had lost his patience and was already backing out of the driveway when Chang arrived home. Chang ran up and stopped him just in time. He retrieved Annette's dress. "Wait—wait—wait! Sorry—sorry—thank you!"

As the boy drove off grumbling, Chang walked slowly up the steps of the great pink track house that Leng and Annette had bought. Their friends and relatives back in Singapore all had complimentary photos of this beautiful house. It looked like it had a thousand rooms. It had a white roof and bay windows and lace curtains with tie-backs. Inside, there was a staircase which spiraled around a crystal chandelier suspended with a long gold chain. There was a high-ceilinged living room and a gas fireplace, above which Annette had hung a blown-up wedding portrait of herself and Leng, framed in gold. There were six bedrooms, each furnished in a different color. There were two cars in the garage. Their relatives were all dying of envy.

Whenever he returned to the house alone, Chang would often stop and admire it from the outside and feel a surge of pride for Leng. But he couldn't appreciate the house that day. He stood before it, feeling very small and lost. He looked around him, but saw only the rustling tops of alien trees against a hot summer sky. It was too quiet; the neighbors were all hiding indoors. He lifted the white plastic cover of Annette's dress for a look. It was a high-collared *cheongsam* in the old style: a scarlet silk dress covered with thousands of rustling gold sequins. In his hands it felt like the sinuous skin that some glorious snake had clawed off and left behind. He raised it to its full length and shook it gently. The sunlight caught the rippling light of the fabric and for a while it gleamed deliciously, like an old, old melody.

Chang stared at the dress for a while. Then, still unnerved, he bent and took off his shoes carefully, knocked them against the doormat that said "Welcome", and entered the dark interior of the beautiful pink house on stockinged feet.

LIONS IN WINTER

IT WAS THE WORST blizzard that the New York metropolitan area had seen in a long time.

"Happy Chinese New Year!" came the voice over the phone.

It was my big sister, Francesca. Yes, that was her name. Pregnant women being the capricious terrors that they were, my sister's fate was sealed one afternoon, back in the 1960s, when my expectant mother walked into the movie theater to escape the heat and saw a film about a dolphin called *Flipper's New Adventures*. The lead actress's name was Francesca. I used to joke that it was better than being named after the dolphin. Francesca's other name was Bee Geok, which she hated.

"Hello, Francesca," I said dully, squishing the receiver against my shoulder at the same time as I was typing away at my keyboard, trying to finish a paper.

"So, what are you going to do to celebrate today? It's the first day of the New Year!"

"So? It's not a public holiday in America."

A shriek. "You still have to go to school? That's not fair. Is there any atmosphere? Any festivities? Maybe in Chinatown?"

"Francesca, I hate New York Chinatown, OK? And it's snowing like crazy. Classes have been cancelled and I'm not going out of my apartment."

That was when she lobbed over her Scud missile.

"But you have to go to out today, I just called Uncle Jimmy and told him that he has to take you out for Chinese New Year dinner!"

My heart sank. Francesca was always full of plans for everybody. Ever since our parents passed away, she had been running my life. It was worse than having parents. But I was supposed to be grateful, for, as was family legend, *She gave up the opportunity to pursue her studies for the sake of raising her little brother.*

"Who is Uncle Jimmy?" I asked rather fearfully. "This isn't one of your arranged marriage set-up things with parents pushing their daughters at me, is it?"

It turned out to be much more cut and dry. "Uncle Jimmy" was the husband of the woman who looked after Francesca's kids in Singapore. He had been living in New York for nine years, supporting his wife and kids back in Singapore as a cook in a Chinese Malaysian restaurant in Flushing, Queens. Could I go and meet him today because he was going to treat me to a big festive dinner in Queens at his restaurant.

"Fran, Flushing is hours away by train," I said, looking out the window. "It's in *Queens*. That's like, another country, man. What's the big deal. I don't even know this guy. I hate how you are always trying to make friends for me on my behalf."

"I thought Flushing was in New York?" squeaked my sister.

Like most of my relatives, she was hopeless at understanding American geography. She refused to grasp how large the country was. She once tried to book a hotel in Albany, New York, in order to come visit me in Manhattan, thinking that it was all in the same neighborhood. I explained that going to Flushing was like going to Sentosa all the way from Woodlands. At least, that's what I guessed. The fact just bounced off her.

"What's the real reason, Fran?" I prodded. There was always something in it for her. She didn't just make long-distance phone calls for nothing. It turned out that Uncle Jimmy had, at her request, purchased two large packets of Chinese herbs which I was supposed to pick up and bring back with me during my next trip back to Singapore.

"You're kidding me," I said sourly, touching a fingertip on the icy windowpane and wincing. "Heard of Fedex?"

"It's cheaper if you just pack it in your suitcase and bring it back, Freddie. Please. Please."

"Francesca, you can buy Chinese herbs in Singapore."

"Yes, but I heard that they're *cheaper* in Flushing."

"I do not understand the cost mechanics of this process. How much cheaper? Is the savings even commensurate with the cost of my train ride to Flushing, and a potential taxi ride back to Manhattan since it's freezing?" I was irritated. The last time I went back to Singapore, I had to bring back four Louis Vuitton bags for Francesca and her mahjong gang because, they heard, it was *slightly cheaper* in New York. They had not factored in sales tax.

"Freddie, you're always so selfish. Just like our father. Daddy never liked to bring back things for me from his trips. Every time Mummy and I ask him to buy something on my behalf, he would scream and scream. I don't know what's wrong with you men. Your brother-in-law is exactly the same."

Because she was, after all, my sister, I finally agreed. I dug out my thickest parka ("L.L. Bean Penobscot Parka: Guaranteed to keep you warm at up to -20°F"), put on my duck boots, stuck ski gloves on my hands, put on a polar fleece muffler and headband, and ventured out into the darkening ice planet. All I needed now was a Tauntaun.

I had lived in Manhattan for nearly three years as a college student, and I had never ventured into Queens. That wasn't snobbery on my part, for you would find people in Queens who soundly declared they never had to go to Manhattan for anything. New York was a balkanized world, and I liked it. I liked how the three boroughs of Brooklyn, Queens and Manhattan were entire big universes in themselves. In general, I found myself strangely drawn to the geographic diversity and the seemingly illimitable expanses of America. And this is all before I ever saw the Midwest and the prairies. I had friends from England who felt the same way. "You could fit all of Britain into one or two states!" they would often point out rather excitedly.

So Queens was a universe of its own, and Flushing was the Chinese universe within Queens. There were some places where there were only Chinese signs as far as the eye could see. You wouldn't know you were in America.

"The Taiwanese businessmen, they fly to JFK Airport in Queens, come straight to Flushing, stay in a Chinese hotel, do their business, then fly straight back to Taiwan without ever seeing any other part of New York," said Uncle Jimmy proudly.

He was a tall, wiry Chinese guy with dark, somber eyes. He was tanned and there were lines around his long face that suggested a hard life in the heat of restaurant kitchens. All along his bare arm were brown stripes and spots that I later realized must have been innumerable burns from being a cook. He had also invited a couple of his other friends for the dinner at his restaurant, so I found myself rather uncomfortably wedged between a young Taiwanese woman with permed hair and a tanned young man wearing huge jade rings who said nothing but simply chain-smoked dourly throughout the meal. Being very Chinese, they did not bother to introduce themselves, but Jimmy introduced me to them as, "my friend's brother." They just nodded.

"This is your sister's," said Jimmy, heaving over two large plastic bags.

I volunteered to pay for her purchase, but Jimmy waved it away.

"No, no need! Your sis is very good to my wife in Singapore. This is nothing."

He had a gruff, Singaporean accent and carried himself with a bold air. In Singapore, there were men like him who sat around hawker centers at night over a Guinness Stout and a cigarette—men who wore open-necked shirts and small gold chains around their neck. They would sit for hours at a time, then grunt an observation, tap the cigarette on the ashtray, and shake their heads. I often wondered what they talked about. Politics? Life? Family obligations? Horse racing scores? Their world seemed incorrigibly macho and alien to myself.

Jimmy had prepared some homestyle Singaporean dishes—*laksa*, *char kway teow*, pig stomach soup with white peppercorns and salted mustard greens. When speaking of his cooking, Jimmy became inexplicably tender.

"I love salted vegetables. I'm Teochew, you know. How do you say that? *Chaozhou ren*." he said, winking at the Taiwanese woman on my right. She rolled her eyes and said something in crisp Mandarin about

45

Teochew people being so poor that they had to salt their vegetables and pretend it was meat. The man with the jade rings parted his lips in a silent laugh.

It turned out that Jimmy's cooking was wonderful, just like the real thing. It was worth the train ride and having to share the meal with utter strangers. I was just helping myself to more soup when I heard a shout. Some restaurant customers were up on their feet and looking out the window. I heard that unmistakable rhythm of the Lunar New Year: the brassy crash of Chinese cymbals, the quickening thud of drums. A lion dance troupe was performing rather bravely in the blizzard outside. The performers were a mixed bunch of Asians and African-Americans, the latter looking rather incongruous in Chinese dance troupe costumes. A banner proclaimed that they were a youth troupe from a Queens community center. The only criteria for entry appeared only to be enthusiasm and athleticism.

A couple of NYPD cops stopped in their beat to watch the show. They were enraptured; they did not expect color on a dull winter evening. High winds lashed against the trembling lion and caused the banners and flags to snap and stutter. From the distance came the stutter of firecrackers. It was illegal to set them off; the culprit fled quickly. Only the ensuing fragments of exploded red paper, borne in the wind towards the lion dance, betrayed the crime. They swirled madly in the wind, mingled with snowflakes, then fell like bright confetti on dark hats of the astonished cops. One of the cops took off his hat to dust off the scarlet fragments, pausing to pick one up and sniff at it. What did he smell? I wondered. Gunpowder, fire, the lost dream of spring? I saw him tuck the fragment into his pocket: an astronaut pocketing a moon rock. Didn't he know that in that brilliant color lay the fervent, collective hopes of the Chinese? Our desperate hopes for money, for wealth, for blessings, for relevance in this cold, wintry land? The lion dance was over. I watched as the policeman and his colleague walked away slowly, side by side, resuming their patrol.

"*Gong hei fatt choy!*" said a fat little man to me, and gave me a red packet.

Jimmy said that that was the restaurant owner. He was proud to show me off to his boss.

"Studies at New York University, you know? It's a big university here. Very hard to get in." The fat little man said something back in Cantonese, which I did not understand.

At the end of the meal, when we were all slurping some *ice kachang*, Jimmy lit a cigarette and surveyed me intently. Then he sighed.

"I had a hard life. No skills, no university degree. If only my two children can grow up to be like you, I will die happy. But my two sons, they take after me. Never want to study. Your sis is a nice lady, she gives them books to read. But I think they're not going to make it. If they can't get a good degree in Singapore next time, they're finished, right?" He tapped the ash off the cigarette on the ash tray. "Our family, we don't breed smart kids. Lousy genes. Not like your family. My wife complains. I tell her, you ever heard of this Chinese saying, dragons will bear dragons, and phoenixes will bear phoenixes? How to expect our type to bear clever children? She and I, we didn't even go past Secondary Two."

"Well, your kids are only in primary school, it's too early to worry," I said. Because I didn't know what else to say.

The snow had not let up, so after the meal I lugged Francesca's precious herbs out to the sidewalk, shivering, and climbed into a taxi. All the way back to Greenwich Village I wondered why Jimmy had to leave Singapore in order to find a job. Couldn't he work at a hawker center or something? Was he in trouble with the law? Was the money really so much better that he would live abroad for nine years, away from his family? Was it really true that there was no future in Singapore for him? I guess I would never know.

I remembered the red packet, and opened it. In it was a crisp twenty-dollar bill from a stranger whose face I had already forgotten. It was a random act of kindness, and filled me with an unexpected warmth.

*ॐᎧ

I forgot all about Jimmy until spring break. While my college friends were off to Cancun for booze and sun, I was forced to return to my own native tropical island. Francesca said my grandparents really missed me. Since she offered to buy the air ticket, I caved in. Besides, her Chinese herbs were really stinking up my apartment, and I was glad to be rid of them.

I hadn't been back for about a year, having spent last summer interning at an investment bank and making some good money. It was strange to get off the plane and enter the tidy confines of Changi Airport. I blinked at the placid, fluorescent light. The ochre tiles, the potted orchids, the Malay immigration official who processed my passport, tidy and scrupulous in her bright pink headscarf—"Want a sweet?" she gestured at a patterned glass bowl as she replenished her supply from a plastic bag beneath her desk. I almost burst out laughing; she was so different from immigration guys in the US. I couldn't be anywhere else in the world. And the smell. A warm, seeping, slightly musty smell of earth, tinged with the faintest hint of diesel, which announced that you were in that unique configuration of city and jungle. Savor it, because after twenty minutes your nose gets accustomed to it, and you no longer notice the smell of Singapore, until the next time you return.

When Francesca took me out to the parking lot, the heat engulfed me like a blast from giant bellows. It seeped deep into clothing, causing skin to prick and scalp to tingle. The leaden air sat heavy on my chest and I breathed deeply a couple of times. I could hear Singaporeans around me chattering away in their anxious, accented English, and the slap-slap of slippered feet on the pavement.

Yeah, I was definitely home.

"No, no, give your luggage to Chong, he'll handle it. Chong, go get the car!" twittered Francesca. "Chong, don't drop that bag, it's got my herbs in it! Hurry up, Chong, very hot-*lah*!"

Chong wasn't her chauffeur as one might have imagined, but Francesca's long-suffering, mild-mannered husband of fifteen years. Chong liked to have me back in Singapore because that meant Francesca would get off his back for once and boss me around instead.

We got into Chong's old white Mercedes with faded red leather seats and sped through the night highway, past silent, glowing blocks of flats and warehouses with their new coats of paint, and more, ever more bushes of bougainvillea. My little Lego nation, I thought, looking out the window as Francesca embarked on her usual stream-of-consciousness monologue. And how did I fit in, as a Lego chip? I turned round and tried to pay attention to my sister.

"Tomorrow we are going to have dim sum with Grandma and Grandpa at this new Chinese restaurant, then after that we are going to see Aunty Jenny because you haven't seen her new baby yet, and after that Chong will pick us up from Aunty Jenny's place and take us to this new marina club—he just bought the membership, they have very good *rojak*, you know. Where can you find authentic *rojak* these days!"

Chong shot me a glance, "I didn't buy a marina club membership for the *rojak*."

I winked.

"Then day after tomorrow, we are going to pick up Edwin and Edmund from Mrs Ong's, the kids want to go swimming—oh, by the way, Mrs Ong might want to talk to you, you went to see her husband Uncle Jimmy right? She hasn't seen him for two years so she said she wants to just find out how he is doing. Then after that—"

"Francesca, enough already. Headache-*lah*." said her husband quietly. Francesca ignored him and turned round in her seat, where I was spacing out.

"Freddie! Do you think I put on weight?" she asked delightedly.

"Of course not." At least, that was what I wanted to say, but since I was back in Singapore, I lapsed into our beautiful patois. English seemed too officious, too cold, for our tropical clime. I was among bougainvilleas. In Singapore, if a woman asks if she looks fat, you say, with a reassuring drawl, "No *laaah*, where got?"

That, of course, was the only acceptable answer to such a question from Francesca.

❧

Francesca's twin sons, Edwin and Edward, didn't really live with her and Chong. They were only four years old, and it was not until they were seven that they would be lucky enough for the "homecoming." It was fairly typical for Chinese Singaporeans who could afford it to contract out childcare to "foster nannies"—Chinese women who choose to make money by minding the children of others in their own homes.

The nannies were usually a notch below their employers in social class—middle-aged women who did not complete high school. Some were illiterate. Fostering helped them to supplement their husbands' income. "After all, I have to stay at home and look after my own kids anyway," they would say, "Another one or two kids would not make a difference." They didn't have to pay income tax either, as they were paid in cash each month. As Francesca had once assured me, it was a "win-win" situation. She thought it rather strange when I told her in America, only orphans or kids who were abused by their parents live in "foster homes." Francesca said foster nannies were the ultimate in convenience. "How else were we going to get any sleep when they kids were born?" she would say. "How would Chong manage to go to work every morning? Look at him, you think he can stand to hear a baby go *nyah-nyah-nyah* all night? Don't forget who we are talking about!" I noted that in Francesca's world, every sacrifice was always allegedly made for the menfolk.

Thus, Edwin and Edward got shuffled off to Mrs Ong's after they were born. There they would remain until it was time for them to attend primary school. Francesca visited them on most evenings, and they get to come back to Francesca's and Chong's rambling old bungalow on weekends. They viewed spending time in their own homes as some sort of special holiday, because their parents would usually lavish extra attention on them to make up for neglect during the week. Special excursions to the shopping mall for toys, or to the country club for swimming, were the order of the day. The boys often cried on Sunday nights when they were returned to their foster nanny. I told Francesca that the whole arrangement was, for the kids, what the Americans would call a "mindfuck." She told me to watch my language.

Francesca never swore: whenever tempted to use the F word, she would say "fish" instead, a habit I found very amusing.

"Call Uncle Freddie!" barked my sister, when the kids greeted us at the door. We had arrived at Mrs Ong's flat in a quiet housing estate not far from Francesca's home. I had a big box of old children's books in my arms that Francesca had purchased from a used bookstore.

"So this is your brother!" said Mrs Ong. She was a tired, thin woman in her late thirties with permed hair, in a big Tweety Bird T-shirt and a pair of black leggings. A very pleasant half hour passed as Mrs Ong brought out some orange soda in flowery glasses and some cut fruit with toothpicks inserted in each slice. I had almost forgotten what it was like to visit a household like this. In America, nobody ever brought out anything for the guests when you visit. Maybe a can of soda, or some coffee, but you were lucky to get anything else. In Singapore, the more old-fashioned like Mrs Ong always offered cut fruit, or a blue tin of Danish cookies, or a box of Van Houten mixed chocolates. I remembered a great-aunt who would always send her kid to buy a *pandan* chiffon cake from the bakery downstairs whenever we visited, no matter how mundane the occasion. In America, hospitality could swing wildly from the informal to the extravagant. In contrast, the plate of cut fruit offered by Mrs Ong spoke of a formal yet modest hospitality that moved me deeply. She seemed to belong to a simpler time.

I picked up my nephews and held them upside down, which proved very popular. Then Mrs Ong's two sons came out of their dim bedroom and had to listen to a long lecture from Francesca about the merits of reading "story books." They smiled shyly and giggled when Francesca showed them the box of books.

"Wah, so many, cannot read finish!" said the elder boy softly, marvelling.

Francesca said loudly, "No, you don't say that. You say, *Cannot finish reading.* You have to speak proper English!"

Mrs Ong thanked Francesca profusely for the books and I could see my big sister puffing up. I guess having done such a good job of "bringing me up," she had now extended her evangelism to the rest of the little boys in the world. For all her preaching about the advantages of cultivating a reading habit, I had never seen Francesca pick up a novel at her age. You would more likely find her getting a facial in her spare time. If challenged, she would assert that "it was more important for boys than for girls"—"it" being a good school, career, prestige, intellectualism, a brain, et cetera. I had no doubt that if Mrs Ong had the misfortune to have borne two little girls, Francesca wouldn't be showering them with gifts (secondhand or not). It was clear that to Francesca, who was very picky with her friends, believed the Ong family still "had hope."

"Yeah, Freddie went to see your husband! Didn't you, Freddie!" she was saying.

I informed Mrs Ong briefly of the dinner and assured her that her husband was looking quite well.

"Has he lost weight?" said Mrs Ong, tearing up.

"Oh, I don't know, he seems all right, don't worry," I said vaguely. I reckoned that a man like Jimmy probably was always that scrawny.

"Did you meet his friends?"

"Well, I met the boss of the restaurant. A Cantonese man, very nice. There were two other people at the dinner—a Taiwanese woman and this guy, I really don't know where he is from, he was very quiet."

To my utter surprise, Mrs Ong turned to Francesca and let out a cry.

"I knew it! He is still with that Taiwanese woman!" Her eyes turned red and swelled up with tears.

"There, there," said Francesca soothingly, patting her hand. The children stopped in their games and stared.

I looked frantically at Francesca, gesturing, "What?" A horrible feeling seeped over me. She was crying buckets now, and her sons slunk back into the bedroom, afraid.

My sister was saying briskly, in the same tone she used to correct other people's English, "Mrs Ong, as I always say, a man is a man. A man cannot be expected to live overseas for so many years and not have the company of a woman. It is only natural that he took up with her. I mean, be realistic. He is over there, breaking his back earning money for you and your boys. And you are over here, thousands of miles away. He sacrificed so much for all of you, and he must be very lonely over there with no friends. If he found somebody to take care of him, you should be grateful. Then he can really concentrate on making money. If he didn't have her, maybe he would have turned tail and fled back, instead of earning money in America. We have to be realistic. Men are men. He has his needs, after all—"

Mrs Ong said, "He promised to send for us the moment he got his green card! But he still hasn't gotten it after so many years! It's been nine years."

"Well, with this kind of thing, it's hard to say, the green card process is very tricky. Maybe next year he will get it? You never know."

"I'm so sick of waiting! All my relatives act like I don't have a husband, that Ah Song and Ah Kim don't have a father!"

"Mrs Ong! How can you say that! We women must be patient—"

At this point Edwin and Edward trotted over to met and whispered that we should play a game, so I excused myself and said I would take them downstairs to the playground for a tumble. Clearly, the two women had no use for me there, and Francesca's gender politics could be unbearable.

I was relieved to leave the stuffy little flat. There was a small playground nearby that I had spotted on the way up, with a sandbox, a slide, and some swings. My nephews took turns on the swings. It was early afternoon on one of those special days in Singapore when the sun was tucked somewhere high up in the clouds instead of beaming down mercilessly on hot heads and hot backs. A rare breeze made its way through the tall housing blocks. In Singapore, the air was often so still that the slightest hint of wind was sufficient to conjure up thoughts of adventure.

Above me, I spied a woman hoisting a bamboo pole of wet laundry out to dry. The clothes flapped in the wind like little flags. It was very quiet—the magic hour before the school buses start trundling in to dump off kids who had finished the morning session and to pick up kids who were in the afternoon one. The light, the air, and the flap of laundry reminded me of the long, cool hours of the afternoon when I was little.

Before my parents bought the bungalow, we had lived in a housing estate like this one. Francesca was in primary school, and I was just a toddler. I remember looking out of the window, twenty floors up, at the world of the housing estate and the kids in the playground and the neat young trees in rows and the snaking concrete paths. I would just look out of the window all day, with my hands curled around the warmed bars of the window grate, until Francesca came home from school. Sometimes my mother would make a kite for me out of a plastic bag, tied to a string, and I would launch it out the window on a breezy day like this one. Beyond my bobbing kite, the housing estate world seemed full of adventure.

It was very strange indeed for me to come back to such a place, after the hurly-burly of New York City. It was like climbing into an old closet that you had hidden in as a child, and feeling the familiar corners. Like Goldilocks, we pronounced this world too small, but the next world, perhaps, was too big. I could never get used to spending the Lunar New Year in snowstorms, to the luxury of red packets in American dollars. And yet I could not fit into the Singapore of Francesca, of Chong and his marina club membership, and Mrs Ong with her heartbreaking sadness in her Tweety Bird T-shirt. I wondered if Jimmy would ever return, and I wondered about my own plans after graduation. Why do we constantly turn our prows to distant shores? When do we know when to leave, and when to return? Could we really, really bear to leave those we knew behind, even if we no longer loved them?

Too hot, too cold. One had to find a world that was just right, I thought, watching my nephews launching their swings blithely in the wind.

THE HAIR WASHING GIRL

WHEN MINA WAS IN kindergarten, they taught her the Chinese characters for country: *guo jia*. The first was an ideogram shaped like a squat box, with a little piece of jade inside. She remembered sitting on the floor and watching as the teacher drew a solid chalk circle on the blackboard, with four thick, formidable walls, like the Great Wall, hemming the precious treasure within. The second character, *jia*, was synonymous with the word for family. This one, Mina thought, was rather like a big shrimp wearing a hat. The teacher wrote it quickly, beautifully—a critter with five sprawled legs and a curved spine. It was completely different from the first character. *Guo* was rigid and respectable; *jia* all wiggly and alive.

When Mina was older, she learned another word that astonished her, because it was an even bigger and wigglier version of *jia*. If *jia* was a shrimp, the word for destiny, *yuan*, was a big spiny-backed lobster. It bristled with even more points and feelers and legs. *Yuan* positively leaped off the page.

She found herself thinking about family and destiny a lot these days as she tended to customers in the little hair salon in Chinatown. A lot of her customers were Cantonese Chinese from Hong Kong or Guangzhou. They had come to New York speaking very little English. They called her *jeh jeh*, "elder sister." *Jeh jeh*, the old ladies would beckon, their hands reaching out slowly towards her. The term confused her a little, since she was not Cantonese and struggled to understand them. Why would older women call her "elder sister?" Her co-workers explained that it was a term of endearment, a show of respect for a stranger. Mina had previously operated in English-speaking Singapore, where strangers were hailed as "Miss," "Ma'am," "Sir." The Cantonese world was one in which the village was still psychologically intact; everyone operated on terms of presumed familiarity; everybody was potentially a relation.

"Elder Sister, what are your opening hours today?" "Elder Sister, which way to the Golden Pagoda shop?" Even rock stars were part of your family. When Leslie Cheung, a famous pop star in Hong Kong, killed himself, all the girls in Chinatown crowded into Mina's shop to watch the wake on television. "*Gor gor! Gor gor!*" they sobbed. Cheung's nickname, known to the Cantonese Chinese the world over, was "Elder Brother."

Many of her customers came in for a perm, although Mina knew that the world beyond Chinatown — the glassy, frosty world of uptown Manhattan, which she had only seen in magazines — had probably moved on. Nobody in uptown Manhattan would be getting a perm these days, Mina decided, as she carefully applied setting lotion on the salt-and-pepper curls of Mrs Wong. Sally, the Chinese American student who came regularly to her salon, said that only Asians would be ashamed that their hair didn't have body and want to curl it so badly. Sally said that in New York, the richest, whitest people had stick-straight, flat hair, cut to a blunt bob. The richer you were, the more timeless and featureless your hair, said Sally. Rich white people had hair that looked the same in any era. Number one: it had to be very, very flat and straight, and number two: it had to be very, very golden. Look at JFK Junior's wife.

"Who's JFK Junior?" asked Mina.

Sally explained, "I was at my boyfriend's house in Long Island the day he died. I can't believe it, I lost my virginity the same day John-John died! Isn't it *totally* weird?"

Mina smiled at the memory of Sally's remark. These Chinese American girls would say anything in public. She reached up to bring the overhead hairdryer down over Mrs Wong's head. She adjusted it carefully and flipped on the switch. It began to roar. The hot air ruffled the magazine pages that Mrs Wong was reading.

"*Gei loi ar?*" asked the old lady, looking up.

Mina said the first Cantonese words she had ever been taught to say, because the answer was always the same for the amount of time for the curls to set, and because the customer always had to be assured that Mina would return to check on the progress. "*Sam-sap fan zong zhi hao, ngor tong lei check-yat-check.*"

"Okay, *mm-goi.*"

When Mina first came to New York, she was amused to find that the little Chinese salon had not escaped the 1950's. The salon had two of those overhead "bubble" hair dryers that you pulled down to fit over the customer's head (redolent with the acrid smell of lotioned curls) and pushed back up when you were done. It also had the electric plug-in barber's salon sign by the door, featuring an endlessly rotating rod, striped like a candy-cane. You flicked a switch when the streets got dark. The candy-cane lit up: yellow and red, yellow and red, yellow and red. On slow evenings Mina almost believed she could hypnotize herself by watching the stripes spin lazily up the candy-cane rod.

Mina arrived in New York five years ago. She had just turned twenty; the hair salon in Singapore at which she had worked closed down. It was the economy, said her boss glumly. The salon was too trendy, the rent too expensive. Five stylists and eight trainees were out of work. One of the trainees was from Hong Kong; he had a great-aunt who owned a hair salon in New York's Chinatown. He heard the pay was good, and they were always short of staff.

"Why don't you go, then?" asked Mina.

"Nah, why the hell would I go to New York?" said the trainee in Cantonese. "My great-aunt says there are a lot of blacks. I'm terrified to death of black people."

Mina wrote a letter in Chinese to the great-aunt in question, who said she would take Mina on and find her accommodation, provided that Mina paid for her own airfare and rent. Mina entered the United States as a Singaporean tourist; she had barely had time to set down her two suitcases in the great-aunt's flat when she had to start perming hair.

Madam Fong, her great-aunt, enjoyed making speeches at her customers and employees, most of which were entitled "Young People Nowadays."

"Everybody complains that there are no jobs today," she sniffed. "Meanwhile I am short of staff in my salon. Young People Nowadays, they don't know how to roll up their sleeves and rough it for a while. My daughters, my sons, all useless! Nobody would come and help. Why does one have children, I don't know. There is money clearly to be made, loads of it, and nobody will come help me."

It was true. The economy in New York in those days was flailing, but there was always a line of Cantonese ladies and young Chinese girls sitting on the bench in Madam Fong's salon, reading Taiwanese magazines and watching the little television on which Madam Fong, in flagrant disrespect for copyright laws, broadcasts the latest Cantonese soap opera videotapes, fresh from Hong Kong. It was a far cry from the trendy boutique that Mina had worked in back in Singapore, with its jazz music and celebrity clients.

But New York Chinatown was adventure. Adventure — it lay in the raucous dialogue from the television set, the chatter of the stylists with their customers, the ceaselessly honking yellow cabs outside, the occasional waft of roast pork from the restaurant next door, the hawkers with their pirated copies of Cantopop, the small bands of white college kids lining up with Chinese families for their Sunday dim sum, the pushcart vendors selling little egg puffs, or fried chicken wings, or misty pieces of stringy, sticky candy called "dragon's beard," the solitary black homeless man who walked by their salon at seven o'clock sharp each day, dragging a plastic bag of dented soda cans, his old gray eyes looking at some distant point in the sky.

Once, a magazine shoot came to Mina's street. All the ladies in the salon got up to look: appointments were forgotten, perm lotions left to set unchecked. There was a photographer barking orders, several thin young women in jeans and holding clipboards, and a boy holding an absurdly large sheet of tin which reflected shards of diamond-white sunlight haphazardly, sending them flying at the traffic, at the pushcart vendors, into the small salon with its still-humming hairdryers. Mina thought the young women with clipboards were all models. She tried to see what they were wearing.

Then, suddenly, tantalizingly, out of the blue, a tall, very tall woman prowled out from behind the crowd like an Amazonian. She towered above everyone else on the grimy street like a superhuman, a pale giantess. She wore a thin silver sheath with a slit right up her thigh and her legs seemed to go on and on, as if she was on stilts. Her hair was bright red and stood like a frozen puff of smoke about her head, her lips were the color of bruised plums, her tiny breasts were visible beneath the see-through shimmery dress. She took Mina's breath away. The photographer told her to jump in the air, and she did, impossibly, on her six-inch stilettos. Up she shot like a comet, again and again, while the photographer clicked away. A crowd gathered. Everyone, everyone around the model looked so short, so dull, so ugly, so plain, so imperfect, so friendless, so forlorn. In front of this speci-men of physical perfection, all else was grotesque.

"So, this is what seeing a model in real life is like," breathed Madam Fong. "They say these girls all come from Russia. I wonder what they feed people in Russia? It's impossible that they can grow so big! It's unnatural!"

Sally, the college student, was there. She came to stand beside Mina. The girls exchanged glances, their eyes shining. The tinselly light from the sheet of tin reflected into their faces, spliced deep into their hearts. That world—that other world that was Manhattan—had come to their streets and scattered its glamor so blithely, so fleetingly, over them, like rice at a wedding.

"Wow," said Sally.

"Wow," said Mina.

Sally sucked in her stomach and stood a little taller. So did Mina. They looked at each other and laughed.

❧

At eight dollars an hour, Mina made more at Madam Fong's salon that she did in Singapore, but the shifts were long and there was nowhere to sit down. She cut, dried, permed, highlighted from nine in the morning till ten at night. The little shop was small: there were only three stations and space for a long bench for waiting customers. There was a tiny alcove near the entrance where Madam Fong sat on a swivel stool, by her cash register. There was an obligatory potted plant and faded color posters of European men and women with outdated hairdos. There were no extra chairs, not because Madam Fong didn't want her employees to sit down to rest, but because there was absolutely no more space. Sometimes, the only time Mina got to sit down all day, in between appointments, was on the toilet seat in the tiny bathroom in the back whenever she had to pee. Her feet ached; her arms ached. She often went to bed and fell asleep dreaming that she was still standing up, her arms still raised above a customer's head, endlessly blow-drying. She had also grown a little deaf from the job.

"There is a reason why your kids don't want to work this job, you know," she said in Cantonese to Madam Fong. The lingua franca of Chinatown was Cantonese. Madam Fong had lived in America for twenty years but hardly spoke any English (hers was still of the "Two dollar! One dollar! Hi! Goodbye!" variety). Nobody had to speak English if they didn't want to in Chinatown. Mina continued, "If I had completed high school, I wouldn't have chosen this trade. Your kids are good at school, they're going to go to college and have office jobs. Big money."

"You're sweet to say that, but it doesn't make me feel better," declared Madam Fong. "I should have retired years ago, if only one of my daughters would take over this business! Just the other day, my eldest said, close it down, Ma. What! I said. Close down the shop! I have an obligation to my employees, my customers. The shop's my family, I can't simply shut down for no reason. I don't understand Young People Nowadays—there is plainly money to be made, and they scoff at it. Oh! But one is so tired, tired to death."

It was nearing ten at night, Mina was helping one of the stylists sweep hair off the floor. Soon, Madam Fong's sister would be coming in the little white van to pick up all of them and bring them home. In Chinatown, the proprietors took care of their own. At ten, eleven o'clock at night, there would be little white vans parked outside each restaurant and each shop, shepherding the waiters in white shirts and black pants, the hair salon girls, the cooks, the delivery boys. One by one, down the street, metal shutters would rattle and slam down storefronts, car doors would open and shut. A shout in Hokkien, in Cantonese, would ring out in the cold air, someone would call out a name, to make sure no one was left behind. The boss would get behind the wheel. Then the vans would purr off, the end of another day.

Madam Fong asked, so why hadn't Mina completed high school? Madam Fong thought Mina was very smart, so how come she didn't go to university? Her boss was in good form that night. She was nearing her sixtieth birthday—an important milestone in the life of a Chinese proprietor—and was feeling very generous and fond of all her "girls."

"My girls," she would say possessively, when customers came in. The Cantonese word for "girl," Mina learned, is synonymous with the word for "daughter." *Loei-loei.* They were all Madam Fong's daughters.

Mina told Madam Fong that she had not been happy in school and had dropped out. She started working from an early age. As she explained, she found herself wondering again about family. Madam Fong was a traditionalist: she loved to preach to her employees about how the Chinese family must stick together through thick and thin. It was a solid, unshakeable concept. The Cantonese word for "family" was *ka.* Madam Fong used the word reverentially, heroically (she had been a Cantonese opera singer before she decided to open a hair salon.) Her wide lips would part, her eyebrows would arch, her eyes would fix on a distant point in the heavens. Cupping an imaginary sleeve of her opera robe with one hand, she would gesture and pronounce, "What are human beings, without ka?" And had she not supplied her husband with a family, with family warmth and bliss, with two daughters and three sons (carried, she said, while she was performing on stage, her pregnant belly sashed tightly to prevent the audience from knowing). *Ka,* she would say. Every man needs a family, every heart needs a home. Without *ka,* we are little boats floating in the ocean, at the mercy of the waves.

And yet Mina understood that Chinese families could be very

61

flexible things. It wasn't always this heroic notion: four stout walls of gray stone, encircling a bearded patriarch, a self-sacrificial mother, an array of children (eldest to youngest, lined up against a wall at the portrait studio, their heights diminishing like a series of steps.) In fact, it hadn't been that way for ages. Madam Fong, reciting lessons learned from her own youth, said that the Chinese family was the keystone of the country, the building block from which a nation is founded; yet Mina knew, from a very early age, that this was not so, that Chinese families were indeed very fluid, whimsical things. She knew that her mother, a young Chinese girl from Indonesia, with long, cool limbs and a head of blue-black hair, had come to Singapore in the early seventies with a man who did not marry her, who asked her to work in a bar in Bencoolen Street. Mina knew that her mother had her when she was only nineteen years old, and brought her round and round to many Chinese families, neighbors, distant relatives, in Singapore, asking if anybody wanted to adopt her. Mina knew this because Mina's adoptive mother, whom she was told to call Mummy, had drilled this into Mina all through her childhood.

"If I hadn't taken her in, God knows what would have happened to her!" Mummy was fond of saying to her relatives, to her neighbors, to anybody who cared to listen. "This girl would have ended up a prostitute, earning her keep with some pimp!" Mummy always reminded Mina that she had been adopted, taken in from the storm—Mummy spoke Teochew, and the word for "adopted" in Teochew was something soft, illicit, illegal even: *por*, the word for "carry." Stealthily, in the dark, someone had gone out and taken baby Mina from the arms of her real mother, and carried her away. Mummy was always the first to remind visitors that Mina was not her real daughter, that she was *por lai chee*, she had been carried back home, and nourished, like a nestling fallen from the top of a tree. "I took her in," Mummy would say grandly, fondling Mina's plaits. "How could I say no? Her mother was practically begging. I didn't want a girl, at first, but I was prepared to be flexible." Chinese families were so flexible, in fact, that one baby passed from the arms of one mother to another, without any legal complications.

Adoption meant having to sign papers, pay fees, keep records; *por* meant exactly that: carry.

Mina did not have a birth certificate when she first came to Mummy and did not know her birthday. Mummy registered Mina at the Registry of Births as her own daughter and made up a date of birth. The name of the father was initially left blank, which made the Registry clerk very unhappy. He asked if Mummy could simply supply a name of a dead relative, because if one left the father's name blank the child could not go to school when she grew up. People would ask questions. Mummy gave the name of a dead great-uncle.

Later, when she grew older, Mina got used to telling people that she was *por lai chee*, that she was adopted. In the Teochew dialect, the phrase always carried a sad tone, everybody knew that there was a sad story behind it: poverty, a nameless young mother, the yielding of one's flesh and blood from a lower social echelon to a higher, happier one.

Mummy was a school principal and had saved enough money to buy a condominium. Mummy was old and never married: she would leave all her money to Mina, she often said. And yet as Mina grew older, it was clear that Mummy regretted taking her in. "I should have adopted a boy," said Mummy to her teachers at school. "My friend chose a boy. He just came back from overseas and got married: fifty tables at the Shangri-La. Why did I pick a girl? What can I do with a girl?"

Mina studied at Mummy's school and did very badly, because everyone—even the teachers—made fun of her for being the principal's adopted daughter. Mina dropped out of school, and Mummy insisted that she find work. "I'm not going to support you anymore, you are fifteen years old. A fifteen-year-old boy could make money and support himself!" Mummy said Mina had grown up and bored her; she was looking to adopt another infant.

"What should I do then?" asked Mina, wonderingly, as Mummy took Mina's school uniforms out of her wardrobe to give to other children at her school, because "those poor children can't even afford to buy uniforms." Mummy said that Mina should return to her roots.

"Your mother used to perm hair in Indonesia, didn't you know? Why don't you go and learn how to perm hair?"

Mummy said Mina had to get a job, because an idle mind was the devil's workshop. She sent Mina to a woman who did perms for a living in a nearby housing estate. The woman's name was Mrs Yeoh and she worked out of her own flat. Old ladies dropped by on long, lazy afternoons and Mrs Yeoh would give them a home perm for about fifteen dollars. Mummy said Mina had to learn a craft since she was no good at school, so Mina stuck with Mrs Yeoh for the next three years, mixing perm lotion in the kitchen sink, washing long, white narrow strips of cotton towel that had the brand *Yangtze River* printed on the ends in shaky red curlicues, and standing next to Mrs Yeoh for hours on end, handing out a hair curler every few seconds, plucking them from a basin of pink and blue plastic hair curlers with black rubber fasteners that were almost always smelly and half-corroded by perm lotion. Mrs Yeoh used home perming kits: each kit had two plastic squeeze bottles of lotion, one for fixing and one for washing out the fix.

After a few months, Mina lost count of how many boxes of home perms they went through. Mrs Yeoh gave her six dollars a day for helping her: one fresh green five dollar bill, and one blue one dollar bill. Mummy allowed Mina to keep her earnings: "Don't worry, I won't touch your miserable pay. But you better realize once you hit eighteen, out you go!"

When she was eighteen, Mina ran into an old classmate from primary school. He worked in a hair salon on Orchard Road. Like her, he had dropped out of secondary school and now temped for a rather well-known hairdresser who was often featured on television. "Come have a look," he offered. Mina tagged along to the sleek salon that occupied the entire floor of a shopping arcade and seemed to contain very little except a couple of brushed aluminum chairs and a tall glass of black tulips. All the staff wore black. She sat on a couch made of midnight black leather and tried not to stare when a famous television actress walked in. She was then introduced to the owner, a little man, also in black. He was very famous. Everybody knew him. It was said that he would only be seen in black and never wore any other color in his life. All his staff had to wear the same clothes.

The hairdresser to the stars looked up and down at her.

"Can you wash hair?" he asked her briskly. "We need a hair washing girl."

She nodded, spoke of her experience at Mrs Yeoh's, and was hired on a trial basis. She was given a black uniform to wear. She was paid five Singapore dollars an hour and was overjoyed. Mummy adopted a new baby boy.

☙

She never told all this to Madam Fong, of course. Mummy was now thousands of miles away, and anyway Madam Fong liked the idea that Mina was a good girl who came all this way to New York from Singapore to make money to support an old, enfeebled mother.

It was harder with Sally. Sally was a college junior and was Chinese American. She had never been outside of the United States and thought that the thick, tacky dim sum in New York Chinatown was "totally amazing." She came once every three weeks to Madam Fong's salon because "you guys are, like, the best deal in New York City for highlights." Mina did Sally's highlights. Together they pondered over the giant chart of artificial locks, each one a different, non-Asian shade, and talked about going more "strawberry blonde" versus "straw blonde." Sally sometimes asked about Mina's family, about Singapore. Sally loved to talk to Mina, probably because Mina was the only one in Madam Fong's salon who could speak English tolerably and hold a conversation. So out came Sally's love life, dating habits, current dietary regime, shopping bargains, complaints about her college, about her college classes, her papers and her assignments and her teaching fellows. Sally always expected Mina to follow her news every three weeks and remember where the narrative train left off, but Mina saw nine or ten customers a day, each with a narrative in her head, and sometimes

65

it all just washed over Mina like a giant wave of words in which she would rhythmically dip her oar.

"So we'll be screening this Zhang Yimou film on campus this Friday, would you be interested in coming to see it?" asked Sally. Mina wasn't paying attention —the mixer girl had mixed the wrong colors for Sally's highlights —so Sally asked again. "Hey, Mina! You've never been uptown, have you? You've never taken the subway uptown? You really should, I'll like to show you my campus. It's cool, there are loads of young people. What about it?"

"Who is Zhang Yimou?" asked Mina, correcting the color and beginning to apply it on Sally's roots. The sharp, familiar smell soared up to her nose and made her eyes water. When Sally explained, Mina said she thought it was rather unusual that they would be showing a Chinese film at her American university. "Would your friends understand it?" she asked doubtfully.

"He's very hip now, everybody thinks he's God!" gushed Sally. "Look, why don't you meet me this Friday at 7 p.m.? Here's my cell phone number, just call me when you arrive at the subway stop and I will come get you."

When Friday came, Mina was very nervous. She didn't know what to wear. Madam Fong said that most of the university students uptown wore jeans and GAP sweaters. All of Mina's clothes were from Singapore, she would "stand out," advised Madam Fong demurely from behind the cash register. She said, "Go to any GAP store. GAP, GAP, GAP, that is what my children wear these days, nothing else. All these American clothes. They look like ABC! I don't even know what GAP means, do you? It sounds obscene. But Young People Nowadays, that's what they like." She rolled her eyes, a little exasperated, a little proud, that her sons and daughters were so American. "Why don't I let you get off early today, Mina? Then you can go buy some clothes. But you must promise to tell me all about your adventures uptown when you get back!"

So, at four o'clock in the afternoon, Mina stepped out of the street, past the roast pork restaurant and the jewelry store (which also sold choice ginseng), past the check-cashing store, past old Mrs Wong who sold fake Prada bags ("Prava"), past the butcher and the fishmonger, past the men selling batteries, spare telephone cords, illegal cable boxes, and used mobile phones. She walked down to Canal Street, then to Prince Street and Broadway to save money on the subway token. She had heard of this place called Soho—according to women's magazines, that was where the real people shop. Instead of a glittering wonderland like she had imagined, it was full of drippy fire escapes, European back-packers, and strange, bare lofts which sold very few clothes. She looked in at some restaurants and saw the prices on the menus in the window. A single appetizer cost as much as dinner for two at a Chinese restau-rant. What could they be eating that was so expensive, she wondered. She looked closely. Candles, wine glasses, serrated knives with wooden handles, baskets of brown bread with white napkins knotted around them. A tall, tanned waiter wearing a long white apron that reached his shoes came out for a cigarette, she turned and kept walking.

She felt very self-conscious but nobody noticed her. She wandered around aimlessly until she saw a large GAP sign. She went in and tried to look for something that was under $20—her budget. She found a navy blue cotton sweater on sale, found that it went with her jeans, and pulled it over her blouse before heading back to the subway. On the way out of the store, she caught a glimpse of herself in the new sweater in the shop window and thought how instantly American she looked. She looked like one of those Chinese American girls, like Sally. It was the same hair, the same skin; what a difference an American sweater made. Mummy would not have liked it.

After the film, Sally took Mina to a diner near the campus. Mina had never been in an American diner before, although she often ate "Western food" in Singapore at coffee houses and pasta restaurants in shopping malls.

"Ham and cheese sandwich please," said Mina to the waitress.

"What kind of cheese?" she asked impatiently.

That really stumped Mina. She tried to remember the kinds of cheeses they had in Singapore.

"Um, Kraft?"

"Cheddar!" said Sally quickly, as the waitress opened her mouth and looked scornful. "She means cheddar."

"What kind of bread?" the waitress continued, rolling her eyes.

Again, Mina was stumped.

"Um, white bread?"

When the waitress left, Mina felt as if she had just failed some kind of test. Sally told her that if she wanted to live in America, she would have to get used to a lot of things, including ordering American sandwiches. There were all kinds of choices that one has to make: white bread, or rye, pumpernickel, whole wheat, five grain, sourdough, or Kaiser roll; and there were cheeses: American cheddar, Swiss, Mozzarella, Muenster, Provolone –

"Wait, oh wait," gasped Mina, laughing. "I can't remember all these words. What do they mean?"

"In America, you don't just order a *ham sandwich*," said Sally, grinning. "You specify what kind of ham sandwich. We have all kinds of choices. Americans love custom-made sandwiches."

"But it's just a sandwich, why so fussy?" wondered Mina out loud.

"How do you order a ham sandwich in Singapore?"

Mina considered. "If you order a ham sandwich, they don't ask you so many questions. It's always made the same every time. You just have to eat whatever they make." Suddenly Mina smiled. "There is a phrase in Cantonese that I learned from Madam Fong. She is always saying it: *You eat whatever kind of rice they cook for you.*"

"Meaning?" Sally did not speak Cantonese.

"You know how she is, always sitting at that cash register spouting philosophy. It means you just accept whatever life throws your way. It is what it is. Take it or leave it."

"That sounds kinda sad, doesn't it?" said Sally, sucking her diet Coke through a straw. "Sounds like my grandma back in New Jersey. The way they go on, it's as if all Chinese women have had the hardest lives, isn't it? All sad and unfortunate and dull and oppressed. Like the film! It's as if we all have sob stories to tell. Don't they know we have

68

made progress? We're not like them. We have choices. It's not *The Good Earth* anymore, Jesus Christ. We're marching out of the darkness."

Mina didn't know what *The Good Earth* was. She didn't always get Sally's references. As Sally chatted throughout the meal, Mina thought, "So this was what it was like to be a college student." They had walked a little around Sally's campus before the film started. It was a dark fall night, and all Mina could remember was a lot of young people dressed in hunter green or navy blue, moving in groups in the lamp-lit darkness, laughing and talking. There were the tall somber facades of these old, old buildings, which Sally said were classrooms but Mina thought they looked more like Parliament House, or a museum, and there were statues of copper now stained green, rising out of wet lawns, like forgotten idols from temples and cemeteries. Mina thought she was on a movie set, and at any moment one would turn the corner and see horses and carriages, women with parasols, a man in a top hat.

She noticed that where the college's buildings lined the public streets outside, the walls rose two or three stories without any windows. The ledges on the building's facade were lined with broken glass and long, pointy wrought-iron bars.

"Is that to keep out the pigeons?" she asked. Sally looked and said, "Oh, I guess. And also to keep out the homeless, the panhandlers. You know, the people from outside."

For some reason, the remark stung Mina. Her mind reeled disbelievingly, and she felt as if someone had plucked her up in the air and put her back down again. For Sally had a look in her eyes that reminded her, all of a sudden, of Mummy.

Mina lived in a small rent-controlled apartment in Chinatown that was owned by Madam Fong's cousin. She shared it with six other girls, two of whom worked with her at the salon, and the others worked at Madam Fong's cousin's supermarket. They considered themselves the bourgeoisie of Chinatown, distinct from the fresh immigrants who arrived daily and who worked as waiters and cooks in the restaurants and who lived above the steamy kitchens, ten to a room, squeezed on rusty bunk beds. At least Mina and her room mates had a DVD player, a television, even a karaoke machine. Once a month they even had a group hot pot dinner, and boiled Maine lobsters and shrimp and crabs, and felt very rich and pampered.

When she got home that night, Madam Fong had dropped by and was making herself some instant noodles in the kitchen. She often played mahjong with Mina's roommates; the other girls had gone to bed. Mina changed into her nightgown and began to unfold the sofa bed in the small living room that served as her bedroom at night.

"Hey Mina, can I make you some?" offered Madam Fong, her thick glasses steaming from the bowl of noodles. "You ate already? What did you eat? What do those white people eat uptown? Steak? Ice cream? Did you have fun? What kind of film did you see? Dirty film?"

Mina explained that it was some film by a director from China, about a peasant woman who was forced to become a concubine to a rich man, and then had a love affair with a younger man.

"It was very tragic."

"Ai!" said Madam Fong. "I don't know why those Americans love these films about old China. Always about concubines, women suffering, adultery, peasants. I tell you, these stories are a dime a dozen. It's not that astonishing, really. Why doesn't anyone make a film about my life? Sold to an opera troupe when I was nine years old, tortured and beaten, traveled all over South East Asia in the forties and fifties, singing for a dime, had five kids and another five abortions, and then we had to come to America without knowing a word of English and open a business, otherwise my children will starve. So what's so remarkable about these fancy films that the Americans go and watch? The director had an easy job! Probably just told the story of his mom's life."

Madam Fong paused by the sink, remembering. A police siren burped in the street below, and a red light pulsed against the kitchen ceiling as the police car cruised silently past. Then she looked up at

Mina and smiled, pushing a tea towel across the kitchen counter.

"OK, I'm done here, don't bother washing up my bowl, just leave it here, I'm off! Good night, see you tomorrow."

At the door, Madam Fong turned and said suddenly, "Hey, don't forget, this Sunday is my big dinner! My sixtieth birthday! Wear something nice. We're going to the Phoenix Pavilion, twenty tables! It's all on my old man." She stood at the doorway in a slice of fluorescent light from the landing, beaming and happy. Mina felt a sudden tenderness for her and wished her good night.

THE TOYS

"**W**HY DO THEY LIKE to put stuffed toys in the back of their cars?" The medication created a thick fog in my head most days. Today was no exception. Mrs Riley was peering through the window blinds she had just snapped open. Piercing light flooded the room. I blinked.

"Huh?" I said.

"These Asians. Immigrants. You drive behind them, and sometimes you see they have dozens of tiny little animals—stuffed toys—lined up against the back. Looking out at you with their beady eyes. Like a toy display in a shop. You know what I'm talking about?" She stabbed her finger against the window out into the street. "It's very curious that they do that. That woman next door's Asian. You can see her car from here. Right next to your driveway. She has them, too. All them toys, right up the back window. Bears, cats, ponies. Strange if you ask me. Strange people. Strange practices."

I reached weakly for the bottle of mineral water by my table and she bustled about and poured it into a glass for me. Mrs Riley had been in Massachusetts for since she was fourteen, but her Irish accent was as strong as the day she arrived. She liked to say "stra-aaange" in that accent and anything she said in that accent was doubly strange. You couldn't help but agree with her.

"What's so strange about that?" I said, coughing. "People love stuffed toys. They make people happy. "

"Not adults."

"Maybe she's lonely." My eyes watered and I wiped them with the corner of the pillow case. "Maybe she's lonely during her commute and she talks to them in the car."

"You don't say!" Mrs Riley lowered her voice, although there was

72

no chance of anyone else overhearing. "She works at the university, you know."

"Professor?"

She shrugged doubtfully. "I don't think so, she doesn't speak English very well."

"How do you know? Ever talked to her?"

"Never. Heard it from the postman when she first moved in." Mrs Riley was an immigrant herself, but loved gossiping about "the immigrants". The new ones, of course. The Chinese, the Indians, the Vietnamese who now populate the small towns of Massachusetts like this one. Opening laundromats, running little restaurants. Filling the public pools on Sundays with their kids. Taking over our university campuses.

Mrs Riley started folding the clothes from the dryer and putting them away in the cedar-lined drawers. The sharp smell of cedar filled the cold winter morning. I loved that smell. I had never noticed that the chest of drawers that my Irish grandmother left us was cedar-lined. When you were sick you really did stop and smell the roses.

"Everywhere you go now, you see the little Asian children and their strange haircuts," said Mrs Riley. I thought she was complaining, but her face softened. "Very smart, they say. I'm fond of clever children, you know. Never had any smart children myself. Why do you think they're so smart? Must be something they eat?"

"What do they eat?" I burst out laughing weakly, as she lined up my daily pills—two pink, two orange, two blue. "Rice?"

"Well the Indian ones, they eat lots of curry. My husband liked curry himself, you know. Before he passed. Never made him smarter." She sniffed, pouring out more water and watching me swallow. "You take all your pills now, don't cheat."

"I never cheat," I croaked a bit and started coughing violently.

"It's bad in the morning," she observed.

"Oh it's not so bad." It was true. I was fast recovering. In another three weeks the doctor would be coming to change the cast. At some point I will be told whether crutches are a possibility. Still, it would be some time before I can go back to New York and my office. It was a pity that I would miss my bonus targets for the last fiscal, but hell. Maybe they would pro-rate me. After all, it was speeding to an IPO roadshow that caused me to be in that multiple car pile-up.

"There he is again, the UPS man," announced Mrs Riley, peering through the window again. "Handsome fellow. Do you think he's Irish?"

"Not every handsome fellow is Irish, Mrs Riley."

She shut all the drawers and got up. "I'll be tidying downstairs now. Would you like some breakfast? An egg? Toast?"

"I can't eat." Even as I said that I knew what she would make me. A soft-boiled egg and two slices of almost blackened toast, cut neatly into triangles. That's what she made me when I was a kid, when my parents were alive. It was good to know that some things never changed. She loved the fact that I was back in this house, under her care, being her little Sammie again. She had grown so old, I thought, watching her as she picked up the empty laundry basket and frowned at her reflection in the mirror, adjusting stray wisps of white hair.

"I'll bring you some breakfast, and then you can put on the telly and watch your cooking shows."

I was on the ground floor of the house. With my broken leg I couldn't climb the stairs, so she insisted that I had her bedroom while she moved upstairs. Her bedroom was the au pair's room. It had windows that overlooked part of the back yard and the neighbor's driveway. She had this view for over thirty years. Through this window she peered every morning and commented on the different sets of neighbors that have lived in the red house next door with the white window frames, at the different generations of postmen bringing our mail. Shut your eyes in this small town and time stopped.

For half an hour the pain was excruciating and I leaned back in the bed breathing heavily. The doctor told me to breathe in and out, in and out. Almost like someone in labor. I edged up against the window and looked out, trying to see something, focus on something, to take my mind off the pain.

The neighbor—an Asian woman—not sure if she was Japanese, Chinese—could be anything—lived alone. She had moved in a few years ago, but apparently had never really spoken to Mrs Riley. Since I moved here I had been bedridden so I didn't really get to see her, either. I was a New Yorker by now. You didn't talk to neighbors.

I would see her sometimes, walking quickly down the driveway and getting into the car. She was about my age, but you could never tell with Asians—she could be double my age and still look my age. Because of the placement of the garbage cans and the juniper bushes in her driveway, she had to back her car right up against the side of our house. So I could see what Mrs Riley had been talking about. In fact, now that Mrs Riley made such a big statement about it, I finally took note. I sat up for a closer look. The back of the neighbor's car had about a dozen teddy bears and puppies and kittens and ducks lined up against the window. They were different brands—they weren't like the Beanie Babies that one of our secretaries collected obsessively at the office. These toys were all from different years, different manufacturers. Probably from Asia.

Waves of blue and purple pain. The pills weren't working. I kept my breathing exercise and tried to focus on the toys through the window. Mechanically, I began counting them. One, two, three. There were seventeen. I counted and recounted them but it didn't help. I shut my eyes tightly and my fingertips turned cold in fear. I thought that I would black out. So I opened my eyes quickly and looked out the window again. I began making up names for the toys.

First bear. Rupert. Of course.

Second—cat. Kitty. No, Garfield. No, this was hard. I thought about calling Mrs Riley for help, but I knew she was clattering about the kitchen and I hated alarming her. I could do this. I gritted my teeth and pretended the broken leg was not part of me, was in the next room.

What is a good name for a cat? Come on. Daisy.

Third—another bear. Casper.

Fourth—a brown monkey. Orfeo.

Fifth—a stuffed toy dog. Toby.

Sixth—another bear—there were more bears than any other animal. This must be a girl bear as it was pink with a white bow. Jemima.

Seventh—

"Here's your toast!" announced Mrs Riley. "Are you all right my dear? You look white. Like a ghost."

I couldn't speak. She sat and held my cold hand.

❧

This was my sixth week out of pocket. Without Blackberry. Without phone calls. I refused to take any calls from work. I still remembered the ingratiating little voicemail that Michael Jameson my senior VP at work had left on the machine (before I unplugged it). *Samantha Holt! Jameson here. I hope you're not in too much pain. Hey when you get a chance, can you give me a call? We're just going through our headcount here and wondering if you would be coming back any sooner, otherwise we have to hire to replace you. You know what I mean. Just—let us know, OK? I'll talk to Bridges about your bonus situation. Take care. Bye.*

My bonus situation? Fuck if I cared. Fuck if I got replaced. I was trying to survive and trying not to think about spending the rest of my life in a wheelchair. I was getting to the point where it hurt to even look at the photos of me Mrs Riley had in her bedroom from when I was a kid, because all I could think of was, I made this kid a cripple. And the pain. All I could think about was the incredible pain of the leg, the ribs, the neck. I was having a Christopher Reeve moment. Was this how Christopher Reeve felt? Would I ever wear normal clothes again? Would I ever be able to go to the bathroom alone again? Or take a shower? Fantasies of a one-shot injection that would make it disappear. Miracle drugs. Maybe cocaine? How could I score some?

That morning, the pain woke me up before dawn and I stared sullenly at the alarm clock as it counted slowly to seven thirty and there was finally enough light to see outside. I pried open the blinds. The car was parked against my window again, as always. But things were a little different. There were fewer toys. I never noticed this before. Where have they gone?

"Does she have kids?" I asked Mrs Riley as she brought in the mail.

"Who, the Asian next door? Don't think so. She's always lived alone, strange girl."

"Well, someone removed the toys. Or moved them. There were seventeen before. There are fourteen now."

Mrs Riley looked out of the window. "Maybe they fell down?"

"Go and take a look."

"I'm not going out to peer into her car!" protested Mrs Riley.

"Why not, you're always peering out of the window."

"Well it's my window. But I'm not going out there to look into her car. It's not polite."

I leaned back against the pillows, tired. "The pink bear, the yellow cat, and the brown monkey are gone."

"No, the brown monkey is there," she said, looking.

"She has two. One is slightly bigger than the other, but they're almost identical."

"My, my, someone has really been spying."

"I can't help it. I don't have anything to do all day, and reading hurts."

"Next thing you know, you'll be having names for all the lil 'uns!"

"As a matter of fact, I have."

She looked at me incredulously, then burst out into a vast whoop of laughter. I laughed a bit, then told her my ribs hurt if I laughed. She wiped the tears from her eyes and asked if I could tell her the names. I refused.

꙳

Two days later, a momentous change.

"Only two left." I announced. "Bouncer and Jemima."

"You don't say," Mrs Riley checked the view. "Extraordinary. Maybe she gave them away."

"I am dying to ask her what she did with them."

"Well, she had an Asian gentleman friend yesterday evening," said Mrs Riley. "Maybe she hid them when he came over in her car."

"What was he like?"

For the next ten minutes we made up stories about what transpired in the house next door last night, chuckling. But there was no fooling Mrs Riley. She made me take my pills and for the rest of the afternoon I hung about in a grey haze, staring at the ceiling and the exquisite contours of the light fixture.

❧

For almost a week there were only two animals in the back window.

"She has her gentleman friend now," was Mrs Riley's theory. "She doesn't need her little animals. Only puts them out when she's feeling blue, I reckon."

Whatever the explanation was, the missing toys drove me into an increasingly frantic state. I needed to count animals, name them. Those damned things had become so familiar that I was dying to see them again. Through those long and boring mornings ripening into afternoons dying into twilight, I had considered those silly cheap toys my friends, made up names, made up biographies for them. Bounce came from a pig farm in the Yorkshire Dales. Jemima was stolen from a teddy bear museum in the South. Annabelle, the giraffe, was from Africa— she was the one who fancied she was above every other animal in the pack. I found it easy to fixate on one particular blank-staring toy, devour the sight of its fluffy head and plastic eyes, and make up stories about them as the pain throbbed through my system. Mentally I would grab each one in a fist and hold on to it and squeeze it and hurt it until the pain went away. Fuck, I couldn't just count two toys. Where were the rest?

"Have you changed your mind about watching telly?" inquired Mrs Riley, removing the breakfast tray.

"No, the noise hurts, and watching it silently reminds me too much of the televisions in the office."

Then, on the eighth day, I woke up one morning and there were four animals. The next day, there were five, and the day after that, fourteen. I almost cried in relief. They were all coming back—Rupert, Orfeo, Casper, Amika, Laurie, Pepe, Big Jacques, Little Jacques, Terry, Garfield, Odie. I counted and recounted for the rest of the afternoon, until I fell into a deep, dreamless sleep.

∗

Cast off!

I could not even bear to look at the strange white thing that was my leg. It felt like something the butcher had left out in a wintry field. Almost immediately a new cast was applied.

"Had visitors?" asked Dr. Weinberg.

"No, I can't bear to see anybody."

"If you like we can get you a wheelchair and you can go outside."

"Not ready for that yet. I'm fine, really. It's too damned cold now to go outside now."

"Well, happy Thanksgiving! Stay warm."

"Happy Thanksgiving to you too. Fondest regards to Mary."

I heard Mrs Riley send him on this way and the heavy oak front door shutting. When she came into the room, I said, "Twenty."

Her eyes widened. "Some new ones?"

"Yeah. She must have been shopping. Car's almost bursting with them now."

Mrs Riley went for a look. "It's a nuisance, really. No wonder they're such bad drivers. You can hardly look out of the back window if you have that many toys in it. You could get into an accident like this." She seemed to check herself. Because I was in a bad car accident, for ever after people could never talk casually about car accidents in front of me, as if doing so meant wishing me ill. Life was strange like that. She said, "I wonder if they celebrate Thanksgiving?"

"Maybe we can ask her to Thanksgiving dinner with us."

Mrs Riley darted me a look of pure panic.

"I was just kidding." I said. I slept for the rest of the afternoon while she knitted by my bed. It was a strangely comforting sound, those familiar knitting needles. I loved falling asleep as a child knowing that she was wide awake and right beside me. Nothing sent me off to dreamland faster.

⁂

In the middle of the night I dreamed there was some kind of throbbing red fire. I remember opening my eyes and reaching drowsily for my glasses, but I was so tired that I dropped the glasses on the sheets and went back to sleep.

⁂

"Good morning! Happy Thanksgiving Day!"

"You are not roasting chestnuts!"

"I am indeed," said Mrs Riley. "Your favorite."

"Awesome. I am never going back to New York."

"Your glasses are on the floor again!" Mrs Riley picked them up exasperatedly, then reached to pull the cord on the blinds, then paused. "You'd never guess what happened."

"What?" I reached for my usual bottle of water.

"Here, let me pour that out for you. We had an accident next door." I frowned.

Mrs Riley had a funny look on her face. She sat down on the bed and handed me the glass of water. "The neighbor next door had an accident. An ambulance came in the middle of the night. You must have slept through it."

"What happened?"

"They say she left a note at the university. One of the lab students found it and called the police. Took her own life, they said. It's on the news."

I turned cold. "Someone died next door last night?"

"I'm afraid that's the story."

Already I had a hard time remembering her face. I only saw her from a distance.

"What was her name?" said Mrs Riley. "Foo—Fong—Phan something. She's from Asia somewhere. It's been on the TV all morning. We don't have such things around here. Police will be by today asking questions, no doubt."

"How—?" I said lamely.

"She did it in the kitchen. Gas. Poor soul."

Suddenly I had a light-headed, tingling feeling. The haze of medication lifted temporarily and the room came into focus. The cedar smell of the drawers, the lamp on the ceiling, the lines of sunlight across the blankets on the bed, the subtle trickle of roasting chestnuts from the kitchen for Thanksgiving Day, all had significance. I reached up and pulled the cord to the window blinds so that the light came flooding into the room.

Silently, we both looked out. Her car had not moved from the evening before. But the entire back window was swept clean. Every single stuffed animal was gone.

THE MOVE

PERHAPS I SHOULD TAKE the pomegranate tree with me, she reflected. There was still time.

Madam Teo, 71, was leaning against the parapet of the corridor outside her flat. It overlooked the car park a floor below, with its canopy of *angsana* trees. The boys said they'd be here at nine in the morning, but already at seven she had been ready, packing up the last bits of her thirty-year existence in apartment unit 02-04, Block 14.

"Ma, you are not taking those foot stools!" Tommy had wailed. "They have to be retired! I've sat on them since I was a baby!"

On the faded leatherette tops, faint blue drawings from a ballpoint pen, from Tommy's boyhood when he was really into depicting Ultraman battling Godzilla.

Jimmy had suggested that she donate her wedding chest of drawers to an antique shop in Orchard Road.

"*Ang moh* tourists like this kind of thing," he said, fingering the worn teak exterior.

The day before, Florence, one of her granddaughters, had tugged one of the drawers open and shrieked in delight to find that her baby toys were still kept in the same place. The toys were always kept in the bottommost drawer of her chest, within the reach of little hands. Out of the corner of her eye, Madam Teo saw Florence, now an air stewardess with Singapore Airlines, pocketing some old strings of pink "princess" beads and a wind-up tin chicken that pecked at imaginary rice on the ground. Even though the tin chicken had long lost its wind-up key and could no longer move, Madam Teo could still hear its characteristic *rat-at-tat-tat* sound. As a baby Florence adored the sound. Madam Teo remembered squatting on the kitchen floor, winding it up for her, over and over again. When Florence cried from teething, the

82

tin chicken was Madam Teo's insurance policy against grief. Was Florence happy with her life? Madam Teo hoped so. All those small, unremembered, loving acts from the past, they must count for something. It would destroy her if she learnt that Florence wasn't happy now.

They spent a pleasant afternoon yesterday, fingering the flotsam and jetsam, deciding which to bring to the new flat. The bed went to Third Aunt's daughter. The sofa went to Second Uncle. The coffee table, to the neighbors who had already "choped" and reserved it. Everything else she could take with her to Tommy's new flat. Everything except her plants.

The old lady was vaguely irritated for the first time. It was always the plants that get left behind. Why?

"The new flats don't have big corridors like these for you to lay out the potted plants, Ma," explained Tommy. "I mean, you could take some of the small ones, but those big potted palms and trees, I think you'd be blocking people's way."

So all that evening the old lady, by the cool breeze after the humid day, when it was kindest to plants, cautiously gathered cuttings. Cuttings from the palm with its lingering fronds, from the "water plum" with its upside-down white blossoms, from the bougainvillea—that easy-blooming friend, so generous with its color, that always reminded her of those can-can girls in New World Amusement Park, back when she was dating her husband.

"Too bad the pomegranate has grown so big," said Florence, putting her arms around the girth of the dragon vessel at the base of the tree. "Remember how Melissa and I would wait forever for the first pomegranate of the year to turn red? Did you really have this since before we were born?"

Indeed she did; it was a cutting she took with her when the Government offered the family, along with tens of thousands of islanders, a real proper flat back in 1971. The original pomegranate tree was over six feet, planted in the corner of her old kitchen garden. Well, not her own, she shared that little plot of dirt with six other families off

Serangoon Road. The six families lived together on one floor above a two-story shophouse, and the Teos lived in one bedroom, with a screened-off cubicle for Mum and Dad and three sponge mattresses for five kids.

Madam Teo had been a seamstress then, the kind who transformed ready-cut fabric patterns into five-pocket denim jeans for a famous Chinese department store. She did it from her sewing machine at home, at night, after the kids went to bed. Every morning, her third son Eric, who was about seven or eight then, would be responsible for shouldering a bundle of jeans she had sewed the night before to the drop-off point, and picking up a new bundle of cut patterns for her. She could still remember his little form struggling under the bundle of cloth, weaving through traffic. She would repay him in her next life, she always thought.

Eric's daughter Cynthia was now a lecturer in a law school in America. Every now and then Cynthia would call her grandmother from that strange land whose night time was Singapore's day time, and whose day time was Singapore's night time.

"Ma," she would joke, "I'm lecturing today on labour laws to protect immigrant textile workers in New York's Garment District. I thought about you."

The old lady would protest gently. "Oh, in my time it wasn't that bad. They paid about 50 cents per pair of jeans. That was good money then. Of course, nowadays people deserve better. Nobody should be doing that kind of work."

"They still do!" said Cynthia. And proceeded to tell her about Mexicans, Chinese workers in America. Their hopes, their sacrifices. Cynthia was a bit of an activist. Madam Teo was very fond of her. She never could understand why Cynthia studied so much just to help illiterate people in a foreign country, but she was glad that the girl did. Madam Teo didn't know how to read. She knew that all she could do was to contribute to life the labour of her hands, the fertility of her body. She knew very well what was fuelling the souls of these immigrant men and women in faraway America, even though she had no idea what a Mexican looked like.

Beneath her, the coffee shop was bustling with the breakfast trade. She could smell steam from *char siew bao*, and the occasional humid waft of *nasi lemak* coconut rice from the Malay stall. She wondered if the boys would be hungry when they arrived with the lorry. All they, and their wives and kids, ate these days was food out of cans and boxes. They even drank out of boxes. Like astronauts.

In some ways she was not sorry to leave her old housing estate. The wet market had been scaled back. They'd stopped selling live chickens on the premises—the Government said it was unsanitary. And Ah Goh of the famous beef ball *kway teow* soup had retired. His stall had been rented out to a young, churlish hawker whose rojak was quite rubbery. Thrown together like fast food, the chilli from a supermarket-bought squeeze bottle, not home-made. He didn't know the real stuff. Madam Teo did. Her father had been a street hawker.

Just as she was wondering how to fill her son's stomachs when they arrived, her wok having been shipped off to the new flat two days ago, an old goods lorry trundled into the parking lot. Someone honked and waved a bare arm wildly out of the window. She watched Tommy disembark, followed by Jimmy, and Tommy's two teenage sons.

They were talking about soccer when they slapped their flip flops up the stairs.

"Ma! Ready for some action?"

First went the dining table, carried upside down like a strange beast shouldered off for slaughter. Then a couple of spare chairs, folded up. Then bags and bags. And boxes upon boxes. A seemingly endless stream, all carefully tied with string. At the end of the parade came an odd assortment of things she threw together at the last minute after she ran out of boxes. Slippers. Bamboo poles for clothes drying. Shower curtains, still damp.

To each of the boys' questions, "Why take this?" she answered, "Then you don't have to buy a new one."

"Ma, this cheapo ash tray is only a couple of dollars at the most. Can't you can leave it behind? We've had it for forty years!" Jimmy exclaimed, showing it to his nephews.

85

"No, no, keep, keep!" said his brother. "Antique! Antique!"

The four men made short work of the move. Within an hour the lorry was loaded to the brim. It was curious to see her belongings in the full light of day, pulled from the blue darkness of her two-room flat, like mushrooms unearthed and exposed to air. Exposed to the eyes of curious passers-by (every move is interesting, arouses the same feelings in everyone), to the eyes of breakfasting old men in the coffee shop who followed the progress as if it was something on television.

"Ah So! You are finally moving!" called out the old *Ah Pek* who sold coffee at the coffee shop (hence, "Kopi Pek"). "Take care in those new-fangled housing estates! I heard they have those new types of automatic trains that go above ground on sky bridges—with no drivers! Scary if you ask me!"

Madam Teo blushed and murmured that she was proud to move with the times.

"The Government must have tested them to make sure they were okay before they let us ride them!" she said.

Tommy's elder son Boon handed her his mobile phone. "Ma, Aunty Florence on the phone."

Florence apologized from the airport for not being there on the big day. "I'm scheduled to fly back from Sydney on Thursday, I'll come see you all in the new place then!"

"Okay. Be careful in the air," said the old lady, who distrusted airplanes. "Don't volunteer to work extra shifts just to make a little bit more money. It's not worth it."

"Ya, ya, OK."

"I worry about you."

"Are you sad about moving, Ma?" asked Florence. "After all these years?"

The old lady did not expect the question.

She thought about it for a while. No, no. They were just relocating from one housing estate to another. They were getting a new flat. How could this be sadness? Sadness was war, was famine. Sadness was seeing your father-in-law in China lose all his rice fields when the

Communists took over. Sadness was watching your father crawl home after being bayoneted by Japanese troops in 1942. Sadness was watching your pregnant mother contract malarial fever in occupied Singapore, not having any drugs to allay her fever. Sadness was waking up in the darkness finding her not in her bed, going out to the rubber plantation to search for her, fearing, as she had threatened, that she would take a cold bath in the nearby pond. Sadness was finding her drowned pregnant form by moonlight, and knowing that you had to be the one to run home to wake your father and tell him the news. Sadness for ever after was the funerals of mothers that her friends and cousins lost, for which she could never attend, because they reminded her of how she lost hers.

They told her the other day, on television, that Singapore was celebrating its 36th year of independence soon. Someone—one of the younger grandkids—had remarked how short that time was. To her it didn't feel short at all.

Carefully, while the boys were waiting, while the lorry's engine was panting in the rising heat of the afternoon, she snapped off a branch of the pomegranate tree, wrapped some moist tissue around its base, and put it in a plastic bag with the other branches. Which would someday be green saplings potted in new soil. You take what you can with you.

She locked up the old flat for the last time. Smiled a little when she saw that one of the boys had prised the metal door number plate — 02-04—off the front door as a souvenir.

"History, man!" she could just hear Tommy saying to his sons.

Then she made her way downstairs to the waiting lorry and the laughing boys (for they will always be boys to her) and they began trundling northward up the island to a new life.

MRS CHAN'S WEDDING DAY

M RS CHAN SAYS SHE will not be working on New Year's Day. She will not be vacuuming the floor. Chain links of cat hair will build up along the corners and crevices, sifting through the air like ghosts whenever a door is opened. She will not be doing the laundry, and the dryer will tumble round and round, making its groan only known to itself in the long, cool hours of the day when nobody is at home. She will not be emptying the dehumidifiers, whose steady drip dripping will move with the hands of the clock, and she will not be shaking the blankets, the thin one for summer, the thick down duvet for winter.

"I was just going to give you a call! My daughter is getting married this Saturday," Mrs Chan tells me.

She will not be coming to clean this New Year's day, and she comes today only in a special capacity to treat us to *sek paeng*, or "eat biscuits." Not just any ordinary biscuit, for *sek paeng* in this context means wedding cakes. She is doing the rounds! It is an old Chinese custom to bring wedding cakes, and a personal invitation card, bright red with liquid black calligraphy tumbling down the front, to the houses of your friends and relatives. It is a way of announcing an upcoming wedding of your son or daughter. These days people just send "Save the Date" emails, but Mrs Chan has never used a computer. When I hear of Mrs Chan's visit, I am transported back to the 1970's in Singapore. Before Tower Records and MTV. Before automatic toll gates and parents volunteering at elite schools so that their kids could have a place. I am in pre-school, the age of perennially living in my pajamas in my grandmother's flat.

Hong Kong preserves Chinese traditions that died out in Singapore shortly after I started going to school. When children go to school, they

88

lose touch with the small things. The intellectual world usurps the tactile world; the excitement of communication with others replaces the mute contentment of our pre-lingual infant existence. Even as we learn words and thoughts, we lose the immediate reality evident to the child. Yet we have pre-school memories, buried deep and luscious and rare inside the earth, only their tips showing, like white asparagus.

Every now and then, in a fold of life in Hong Kong, I will remember things in Singapore that I forgot to miss, because I didn't even know they were gone. Paper bags with hexagonal bottoms with red-and-white twisty string ties and red Chinese characters on the side. Cork-popping toy guns made of tin. Porcelain congee bowls, called "chicken bowls" because they always bore the same hastily painted red and black rooster emblem on the side. A certain shade of jade green tile and crazy peach-pink porcelain sinks. The thin brown paper that goes around a fresh Chinese fritter. Congee, made in individual batches in small battered aluminum pots over portable stoves. The sharp scent of a Chinese herbal shop. Wedding cake rounds are part of these memories. You excavate them, amazed that they are seeing the light of day.

"I am treating you to eat Chinese biscuits, and Western biscuits," says Mrs Chan, her hair permed like never before, beaming like a new mother. In Cantonese, there are only two diametrically opposed styles: *zhong* (Chinese), and *sai* (Western). Do you want a Chinese meal or a Western meal? Do you want a Chinese dress or a Western dress? Do you want Middle? Or Western? There is no East in the Middle Kingdom, no North. A different compass governs. I, even I in my J. Crew sweater and polarfleece socks, am a *zhong gok yan*, and my white husband, a *sai yan*. By a turn of phrase, we are back in the days of Magellan, of red-haired devils sailing into our precious Middle Earth.

I am disappointed to find that although Mrs Chan personally pays a visit, people in Hong Kong no longer bring the actual cakes. She brings, instead, red and gold-printed gift vouchers for cakes that I have to redeem myself: one for the Chinese cake shop, and another for the Western cake shop.

❧

Still, I remember those hot afternoons, in Grandmother's dim kitchen, when Great Aunt so-and-so (also with a fresh perm for the occasion) brought over a box of assorted Western cakes, or a thick paper roll of Chinese biscuits that came apart in your hands; how they would gossip and laugh and congratulate each other, and talk about their children —every one of them in their turn, from oldest to youngest —while my younger cousin and I would peek into the cake box and secretly make up our minds which ones to eat once the guest had gone.

"I get the one with the cherry," I say when we retire to the bedroom, away from the grown-ups, to begin our usual consultation.

"Which one?" asks Winnie nervously, clasping her hands. "I saw two with cherries."

"The red cherry, not the green cherry."

"But you always get the red cherry!"

"OK OK!" I shout in alarm as she threatens to bawl. I make her a generous offer, "You can have the red cherry. I'll take the one with the chocolate rice all over on top. The all-chocolate jelly roll."

"But I want that one!"

"Why do you always want the one I want?" I shout. "I thought you want the red cherry one!"

Winnie is confused, and tries to cry again. I deliberate between locking her in the bedroom and going out to play by myself, or feigning indifference to every cake in the box, a ploy which usually works. I choose the latter, and we slide outside to be among the grown-ups again, each mentally running through the colorful possibilities in the big square cardboard box with the shiny thin grosgrain ribbon that is impossibly knotted at top speed by the lady behind the counter into a perfect bow. The square one in bright lizard green—the *kaya* cake— the bright yellow mango roll, the silent mauve one with blueberry on top, the virgin snow white rectangle with coconut. The pillowy egg roll with an irregular pattern burnt on its smooth outside that the Chinese bakers call "tiger skin." The dark, exotic smell of cocoa from the chocolate roll, and—the ones that kids don't like because there is no cream on them—the chiffony *pandan* cake and orange Bundt cake.

⁂

Mrs Chan's Chinese cakes turn out to be moon cakes with papery skins that—as is the custom—come apart in your hands. I redeem the Chinese cake voucher after tracking down the Chinese cake shop, Wing Wah, in an old *Chaozhou* quarter of the western district of Hong Kong. The cakes come individually wrapped in modern plastic, with its own silica gel sachet to keep fresh, indefinitely. The Western cake voucher is redeemed at a store called Maxim's "Western Biscuits". The Western cake voucher redeems twelve pieces of assorted cakes, in different shapes and sizes. You get to choose.

"Which ones would you like?" asks the pregnant lady behind the glass refrigerated counter, beaming and posing her stainless steel tongs above the cakes expectantly.

I am a child again. "All the ones with the jam tops. This one, and this jelly roll. More of the orange jam tops." I am happy as a lark. Now that I am grown up, there is no more negotiating or sharing with any other kid in the house. The entire box is mine.

⁂

As I still have to go back to work, I park the cakes in my office communal refrigerator before taking them home. This causes me some anxiety. All day, the box of cakes sit waiting, hidden in my office pantry, deep in the humming refrigerator behind the cans of Coke. As was office custom, I affix the obligatory warning, written on emphatic black marker on a yellow Post-It: "Jean S. Wong's—Do Not Remove!" (which basically meant: stay away from my goods, you bastards.) All day, I rehearse the sight of the gleaming patchwork tops of the cakes, glowing underneath the cardboard.

Where were those cakes of my childhood? Where was Winnie? And

91

Great Aunts and Great Uncles? And their sons and daughters? Where were those marriages now, to whose health and happiness, to whose fecundity and longevity we toasted long ago, by eating sweet cream cakes? When I eat cakes for a new wedding, I remember the faces of proud parents announcing the weddings of the past. Many parents have since died. Even the brides or grooms have died. Others have divorced, leaving confused children. These wedding cakes embody so much hope for the future, and what can we—everyone in this transaction, from the parent, the baker, the cashier, the greedy child who puts the cake in her mouth—do but to hope?

"I wish you could come to the wedding banquet," says Mrs Chan. "You are very naughty indeed not to come, to have to go to another wedding banquet that day." It is a popular date on the Chinese calendar for marriage, the first weekend of the New Year. She holds my hand, as if I am a little child, and swings it to and fro, reluctant to leave. Her hair is ruddy with hair dye, and her muddy grey eyes, flecked with age spots on the whites, look happy with expectation. She says her daughter is my age, and that there will be thirty tables at the Jumbo Floating Restaurant.

"I won't be cleaning this week, so you guys will have to do this all yourself!" she waves a hand over my kitchen counter, and tells me that we are very obedient kids. My husband, who cannot understand much of the half hour conversation in Cantonese that we just had, strays uncertainly by the door. I laugh, she laughs, and I congratulate her again.

"We forgot to offer her tea," he says, after she left.

KENNY'S BIG BREAK

PUBLIC TRANSPORTATION, BEING RELATIVELY cheap and widely available in Singapore, is an integral and unenviable aspect of school life on the island. After one o'clock on a school day, hoards of nut-brown teenagers clamber gratefully into the air-conditioned embrace of subway trains and buses to be shuttled from the internment camp of school to the confines of suburban homes or HDB flats. This forced march takes place twice daily. It certainly would have been mind-numbingly dull if Kenny didn't have a good friend to accompany him. He was most fortunate to have Chee Beng, who could always be counted upon to provide entertainment during the ninety minute ride.

Kenny and Chee Beng were at the age where exclusive male friendships consist of the mutual hurling of verbal slings and arrows on public transportation. If they were still in primary school, they would be shoving each other's knees, or flinging boogers, or dabbing each other with permanent black markers, or taking turns pinching each other to see who could withstand pain. However, with secondary school came puberty and an appreciation for psychological torment. Knowing that there was nothing worse for a boy than to have an older sister, Chee Beng often ripped up Kenny's sibling in public and that day was no exception.

"Ha ha, your sister is marrying an *ang moh*," Chee Beng smirked as they rode the bus home.

"So?" said Kenny. An insolent school boy could perform wonders with the rejoinder "So?" if uttered with the right drawl. In his case, Kenny was attempting to shut up his friend, but to no avail.

"So is your family going to emigrate with the American guy?" said Chee Beng.

"Maybe," said Kenny defiantly. It was true; the issue had not yet been settled. "What's wrong with that? You're just jealous because you can't go abroad."

Chee Beng chanted, "Traitor, quitter, army drifter!"

"What makes you think I won't serve National Service?" said Kenny hotly. "Anyway, so what if I live abroad. Doesn't mean I'm a traitor. Being Singaporean is something larger than simply living in Singapore. I'm not going to stay behind just to prove your stupid point."

"Don't emigrate with your stupid sister. I have a better idea." Chee Beng lowered his voice mysteriously. "I'm going to apply to university in America. I'm going straight after my 'O' Levels. You want to come?"

Kenny stared at his friend in disbelief. After all, the boy had only been tormenting him for the last hour with tedious observations about people who leave Singapore. Then again, he could never keep up with his friend's brilliant mind, Kenny thought humorlessly. Ever since he knew Chee Beng in primary school, the boy had contemplated being an F-15 pilot, a NASA engineer, a film director, the founder of an Internet start-up, the star of a West End musical, a Minister of Parliament, and a celebrity chef. One simply couldn't keep up with Chee Beng.

"Now who's the traitor," hissed Kenny.

Chee Beng wagged his eyebrows up and down suggestively. "I've persuaded my dad to get me out of the country and enroll me in University of Southern California. I'm gonna study film."

"No, *I'm* gonna study film. You're always changing your mind." It was true. Film had been Kenny's consuming passion since he was a kid. He had amassed a large personal collection of pirated videos by the time he was twelve. He saw the original 1977 *Star Wars* sixty-five times. Why would anyone want to be anything else except a film director? he had often wondered. Except, of course, his family wouldn't hear anything of it. He had an equal chance of asking them to sponsor a career in conducting moon landings.

Chee Beng evidently had more success. "I managed to persuade my dad. See, I showed him an article about box office earnings and the profits of the top-grossing films of all time. I showed him that I could make fifty times the profit his computer business makes in Singapore. Wow, that really impressed him! Now he's convinced there's big money in it. I told him that he will make a good return by investing in my education."

Kenny said that Chee Beng shouldn't be going round promising false returns on people's investment.

"Why not," said Chee Beng, as the bus reached their stop. "My brother's a banker. He does it all the time."

They got off the air-conditioned bus into the blistering heat and walked over to the MRT stop to wait for their train. Chee Beng continued pelting Kenny with harebrained schemes. He had it all planned:

• Kenny should persuade his mother to let him go to USC with him;

• They would study film together, then;

• Move to Hollywood and become the next Ben Affleck and Matt Damon.

They got onto the train. Kenny studied the school crowd riding impassively in the serene, air-conditioned space. A toddler was swaying up and down the train. His mother harangued him constantly to get back to his seat. Some primary school children sat in a row of identical uniforms. They were sticking stickers into sticker albums ("What's the point?" wondered Kenny). Outside, the bright window displayed a fleeting cyclorama of trim little trees, white concrete blocks, and a shallow blue sky. It all seemed strangely incongruous against the lurid schemes of Chee Beng.

"Come on, you have to come with me," said Chee Beng, jerking his thumb out the window. "Singapore sucks."

"Well, now that my sister's getting married, my mum can't think of anything else. They've been focused on the wedding preparations for the last six months. I can't really talk to them about it right now." Kenny sighed and shifted his schoolbag against his shoulder. "Margaret's going to move to the East Coast with her husband, anyway. Mum would want me to go study there so that Margaret can—quote —'look after me'. Imagine living near Margaret. A fate worse than death."

The boys agreed that it sucked being the younger son in a Chinese family. Chee Beng said, with the vehemence of a sixteen-year-old schoolboy, that Kenny's older sister was a "real bitch". Several heads turned; eyes flicked to the boys' school uniforms, their school badges. No doubt the next day a responsible member of the public would write to the principal of their highly-esteemed boy's school, complaining of the two boys using the word "bitch" on public transportation. Kenny got into trouble once for criticizing a movie on the bus. When summoned before the principal, he argued passionately that a certain film director shouldn't have attempted a remake of Akira Kurosawa's *Rashomon*, and that the script was poorly developed and the editing was horrific. Saying that it "really sucked ass" should not have been mistaken by anyone for anything other than good, solid film criticism. The principal simply looked fatigued and implored him to preserve the good name of the school, even in film criticism, and try to avoid "words with of crude sexual origin", to quote the letter from a member of the public.

That led the two boys to debate for hours on whether the word "suck" could justifiably be interpreted as being "sexual" in origin.

"I guess so," said Kenny gloomily. "People just have dirty minds."

"But that movie really *sucked*," said Chee Beng.

No, it definitely wasn't easy being a sixteen-year-old school boy, especially if you were constantly emasculated by a fussy mother and an over-bearing, pious sister. Margaret hated Kenny ever since he was born. She often told him that their parents really didn't mean to have him, that he was really an "accident", which explained the eighteen year disparity in their ages. Fortunately, Margaret did very well in school and went off to study in the States after completing junior college, and Kenny was free to grow up in peace. Of all the subjects she could have chosen, she picked Business Administration, which pleased their mother very much because, as everybody says, "it is very practical". Margaret ended up living in the States for many years. She got a job as a human resources manager in a big commercial bank. When Kenny found out what human resources managers did, he thought it suited her bossy self perfectly. The bank was probably full of little Kennys, sweating under her sharp tongue.

And now, at age thirty-four, Margaret was finally getting married to this American guy who worked at her bank. His name was Jonathan Blumenthal and he was forty years old. She quit her job to plan the wedding, and flew back to Singapore to torment everybody and bully them into helping her. When Kenny came home from school that day, after Chee Beng introduced the idea of going to America, he found his female relatives encamped at the big rosewood dining table over a stack of bright red Chinese wedding invitations.

"Aunty Cissy says she is so glad you have found a husband at your age," his mother was saying solicitously. "I was so afraid that you were going to miss the boat. You know, by the time you hit thirty-five, all your good eggs would be gone. The best eggs die first."

"Is that why she is marrying the *botak* foreigner, Mum?" asked Kenny. "What if your babies take after him and have no hair?"

"At least they'll have a good nose," said Margaret's mother diplomatically. "Not flat, like Chinese."

Margaret complained to her mother that "your son is being very spiteful". "I don't know where he learns his manners," said his sister. "At the rate he is going, he is going to fail his exams and end up sweeping toilets."

Kenny pretended not to listen. Margaret had a habit of referring to him before her parents as "your son", as if he wasn't really her brother. They were always having these three way conversations where Margaret would advise her mother, in front of him, what is to be done about "your son". Since his birth, Margaret had been predicting that he would end up, alternatively, a "toilet-sweeper", a "beggar", a "drug abuser", and "someone who works at McDonald's." ("I *like* McDonald's," said Kenny.) She accused him of being "childish", "spoiled", "ungrateful" and—always—"stupid". Kenny told Chee Beng that she had some unresolved Freudian issues, and his friend agreed.

After lunch, Kenny's mother told him not to shut himself up in his room. "Come help your sister," she said. "You're good at math, why don't you help her tabulate the costs."

He slid into a chair at the dining table and pretended to take interest in something which he found, at his age, eminently horrific: weddings. For the next hour he flipped through Margaret's collection of Singapore wedding magazines and demonstrated his irritation at being forced to participate in the preparations by letting forth a stream of desultory comments. How he wanted to "slap this bride's face", how the groom looked like "a real wanker", and how "this all looks like shit to me". To his bored, irritable self, the follies of the wedding industry knew no bounds. He got tired of the endless pictures of wedding couples in pearly soft-focus. He laughed at articles about "the wedding dress diet", which followed the articles about how "foie gras" and "Valrhona chocolate" were "essential" for the bride who aspired to be French. He said, loudly, "Women are so dumb," and hoped that his sister would realize that was meant for her. Every now and then, he would gasp at a photograph and show the page to his family, "Look at this shit! They got married dressed as Leonardo di Caprio and Kate Winslet from *Titanic*! Don't they realize the bloody ship *sinks* in the end and they all die?"

"'Shit shit shit'," repeated his mother, rapping his arm. "Don't always talk like that. You and that Chee Beng. You always think everything is shit. And stop talking about dying. Can't you say something lucky? Your sister is getting married."

Margaret looked at the photograph he pointed to. "But it's so romantic. You just don't know how to appreciate good things." She said that she herself had been planning to sing the theme song from *Love Story* over the karaoke machine at the wedding. Kenny promptly ruined it by asking her if she had ever watched the movie (she hadn't).

"The girl dies in the end." he said.

His mother snapped, "Die again! Stop talking about death!"

"It's OK, Mum," said Margaret. "He's just feeling left out, you see. He's just jealous. After all, I'm going to marry a handsome foreigner and move out of this town."

Kenny pointed out, with the revulsion of a teenage boy with his head firmly on his shoulders, that Jonathan, with his receding hair-line, was not good-looking. He had seen the photos.

"Yes he is," said Margaret defensively. "Mum thinks he looks like Mel Gibson. I think he looks like Ralph Fiennes, Antonio Banderas, and Tom Hanks all rolled into one." The two women giggled.

Kenny said that his mother thought that all white men, even the current president of the United States, looked like Mel Gibson. Then he went upstairs because he was "bored out of his mind".

"I think your son has problems with me marrying a foreigner, Mum." she said crossly. Upstairs, Kenny began blasting his stereo.

"Well, you know what we used to say in the old days," said Margaret's mother, her thick horn-rimmed glasses perched at the end of her nose as she surveyed the guest list for the fiftieth time.

"What?"

"You only marry outside your race because no Chinese man wants you."

❧

As the days passed, Kenny noted that his sister's wedding preparations mushroomed in complexity. Her wedding plans had initially been modest. He heard her talking over the phone with Jonathan, whom he had never met. He heard her agreeing that there was not to be any feng-shui consultation. Or dragon and phoenix wax candles, or red packets of money. Or roast pigs (Jonathan was Jewish and pork was a cultural no-no). "Yeah, I'm not a traditional Chinese girl, really," said Margaret jovially. She glared at Kenny when he stuck his finger in his open mouth and pretended to vomit.

They were going to have a beach wedding in the Maldives, surrounded only by a dozen or so close friends and family. Margaret was going to wear an A-line gown bought off-the-rack; Jonathan was going in his best business suit. The whole wedding would only cost five thousand dollars. It actually sounded agreeable to Kenny. He didn't mind going to the Maldives, he told Chee Beng on the bus ride home, before it disappeared under the rising tides of global warming.

Of course, Margaret's mother prevailed.

There was the argument about "your father in Heaven would want you to have a proper wedding".

And, "you are not setting a good example for Kenny."

"I already told her I was gay," said Kenny boredly. He put on his earphones and read an in-depth interview with Steven Soderbergh in *Rolling Stone* instead of calculating banquet costs from hotel brochures, as he was supposed to do.

"You cannot refuse to throw a Chinese banquet. There are the relatives to consider. Remember what happened to Aunty Patty."

Oh yes, Aunty Patty. Out of the corner of his eye, Kenny saw an unmistakable look of panic flit across his sister's face. Aunty Patty eloped with Uncle Joseph and never threw a Chinese wedding banquet. Although legally married, everyone thought they were living together. When the kids were born the situation was most awkward.

"I think it even affected the kids' chances of getting into the right school," said Margaret's mother. "See how saving a few thousand dollars can ruin the next generation?"

"That was forty years ago, Mum," said Margaret, sounding unsure. "Anyway it's not just a few thousand dollars. If I do it, it'll have to be big. Bigger than all of my friends' weddings. At least one hundred tables."

Kenny reached for the desktop calculator, snatched the hotel price list from his sister, and punched away. "That's over a hundred thousand dollars," he said in disbelief. "You could make an independent film for that amount of money!"

"Oh shut up," said Margaret crossly, snatching the list back. "Anyway, it's a Chinese wedding banquet. You don't have to have the money. You count on getting red packets, maybe you put up 30% of the costs, and get the guests to cover the rest. That's why it's important to appoint my bridesmaids to collect the red packets and guard the money box."

His mother said thoughtfully, "Aunty Mimi's daughter actually made a profit on her wedding you know! So lucky."

Margaret said that she was determined to make a profit as well. She could not lose to Aunty Mimi's daughter. She said she was only inviting the kinds of guests who would give generously. "Since it'll be at the top hotel in Singapore, they'll expect to have to give larger red packets," she said, busily typing into her laptop. She had all her wedding costs saved on a spreadsheet, whose formulas she was constantly changing. "But I'll choose the cheapest menu—the ham-and-corn soup instead of shark's fin—and I figure I'll not only break even, but I'll end up with at least eight or ten thousand dollars extra for my own pocket!"

Kenny muttered something under his breath.

Margaret looked up sharply. "Mum, your son is very passive aggressive. I can't believe you are thinking of sending him to live in the States with me for his college education. I'll be very busy trying to conceive a child of my own. Jonathan and I won't have time for Kenny."

"Whoop dee doo," said Kenny, flipping a page.

"Did you hear that? He doesn't even speak proper English! All he cares about is movies," said Margaret. "Just look at him! What is he good for? All he does is hang out with that Chee Beng and consume CDs and watch movies. You really should control him, Mum. He's getting worse and worse." (She went on in this fashion for a few more minutes, but it would be too tedious to repeat her words here).

His mother and sister began to discuss his university options as if he wasn't there. Kenny realized, with new resentment, that Margaret was cajoling his mother to use "Kenny's money" to finance her wedding. "Kenny's money" was money that his father had left him for his college education. His mother was unconvinced and finally rejected Margaret's suggestion, but his sister's attempt irritated him. The sheer closeness of the escape kept him awake at night.

※

"I don't know, man," said Chee Beng, hanging on to the strap on the crowded bus. "Sounds like she's out to get you. How do you know your money won't be gone if she manages to wear down your mum?"

"Can you believe it!" said Kenny hotly. His young soul trembled with indignation. "What could be more important than your university education? *She* got to study abroad. It's just so unfair that she's trying to cut me off. She's just plain Evil."

"It's all about money, man," said Chee Beng philosophically. "People kill each other over it. My dad is always threatening to disinherit my brother or me whenever we do something that displeases him. I'm lucky he's letting me go study abroad."

Kenny told Chee Beng that at least he had a brother. With a much older sister, and no dad, it was like being ruled by two mothers. "It's bad enough getting bossed around by female teachers at school," he said, depressed. "And then you get home and are bossed around by women as well. What's a guy to do?"

They often had these "what's a guy to do?" deliberations on the ride home. It is unclear how the assumption first arose that single-sex schools offered better education; suffice to say that sometimes the penalty for being too bright was to spend ten years of one's life in a single-sex environment. At Kenny's school, the combination of highly intelligent male puberty with a lack of gender diversity was a volatile one. The teachers were mostly women, on whom the school boys projected a mixture of misogynistic disdain, sexual desire, and violent contempt. Chee Beng was famous for making younger teachers cry by deliberately staring at their breasts when they were lecturing; Kenny got detention once for remarking that their vice principal should really shave her armpit (she happened to be within earshot). Punishment emboldened them, made them heroes in the eyes of their classmates in a subterranean war of the sexes tempered by long, dull hours of rote learning in sun-baked classrooms.

"Women have this anger," said Chee Beng philosophically. "I see it in my mum and my cousins. They're so pissed off that they have to be the ones to have babies, so they have this kind of jealousy at our mobility. It's payback for centuries of male Chinese patriarchy. I swear to God."

Kenny said, in a sudden moment of pure passion, "I haven't met a woman who wasn't a bitch." He felt very daring and relieved at the same time, tossing it out on a public bus. He looked around, but nobody seemed to have heard. He was rather disappointed. He didn't mean it of course, but it sounded right.

"Well, maybe you haven't met Elizabeth Hurley," sniggered Chee Beng.

"Posh Spice."

"Britney."

"Yeah. Imagine if Liz Hurley taught at our school."

"Oh come on, if a woman looked like that, what would she be doing, teaching?"

They got off the bus and walked the straight, concrete path through a field to their train station, kicking pebbles out of their way and trading comments of restless, angry humor.

∗⁕

The feng shui master eventually decided that Margaret should get married in December, just as Kenny was taking his 'O' Level examinations. Kenny had to go over to Chee Beng's house after school to study because his house had been invaded by Margaret's bridesmaids and Aunty Cissy, Aunty Patty, Aunty Mimi, and Aunty Bee Lian. It was wedding prep ground zero. Every day the bridesmaids and Margaret practiced singing songs on the karaoke. The bridesmaids were all from Margaret's church; they planned an *a capella* gospel jam to entertain guests at the wedding. When Kenny told them to shut up, they complained to his mother, who suggested that he go study at the library. "It's your sister's big day, can't you just go along with it?" said his mother, fearing trouble. "It'll be over soon."

"It's really too much," he said over his books at Chee Beng's house. "She's sending a Message. She wants me to fail my exams. That'll prove to my mother what she has always said about me all along."

Chee Beng handed Kenny a copy of the college application. "Got one for you."

Kenny looked through it, depressed. "I haven't talked to my mum about it."

Chee Beng snickered. "You loser."

❧

It was rather unfortunate that, in order for her to fit into her wedding dress (ordered two sizes small), Margaret had to starve herself the entire day and had to toast with cognac on an empty stomach. It was even more unfortunate that she had also committed herself to singing five solos on the karaoke machine during her wedding banquet. The combination of hunger and the exertion of singing made her very dizzy indeed.

It happened right at the sixty-first wedding table. The bride and groom were toasting Aunty Cissy's family. Margaret raised her glass, then simply keeled over. Women screamed. All the guests stood up for a look. The video-photographer wondered if he should continue filming. The *a capella* girls stopped singing "Jesus is Round the Corner" and tried frantically to turn off the karaoke machine.

The groom dragged Margaret into a corner. Along the way, her hair extensions began to uncoil and one of her shoes came off. Her brides-maids and a capella buddies milled anxiously. Guests came over for a look; a doctor offered advice. Aunty Patty brought out her herbal smelling salts. When Margaret came to, she demanded that someone bring her Chinese tea. Then she sat up and burst into tears.

"So humiliating!" she said to her mother, and would not be pacified. "Where's my shoe?"

Aunt Bee Lian came up, looking white as a sheet. She dragged Margaret's mother aside and conferred quietly. *Shtrsh-shtrsh-sheet-shtrsh*, went the women. Their whispering attracted the men, who huddled close. The news began to spread like SARS. In the commotion after

Margaret fainted, the bridesmaids appointed to guard the money box had deserted their post. They left the money box sitting on the guest signing-in desk outside the ballroom. When they went back to look, the box was gone.

There was a big ruckus. Aunt Cissy fainted. The hotel manager was summoned and the theft reported. Margaret limped over the microphone and yelled that nobody was allowed to leave the building. Children began to cry. The waiters asked if they could now bring out the sweet yam dessert as it was fast getting cold. One of Jonathan's Jewish relatives asked Margaret's mother if the yam dessert had "lard" in it.

Margaret had kind of lost it. She was shouting at her husband. The dialogue went something like this:

"I don't have the money!"

"What! You were the one who wanted an expensive Chinese wedding!"

"The guests were supposed to pay for it!"

"You mean you and your mother never had the money for this wedding?"

"I calculated that we could cover it with red packets!"

"I don't have a hundred thousand dollars!"

"So use your credit card!"

"My credit card limit is only five thousand dollars!"

"Don't look at me! I have no money!"

"Well, I don't either!"

Already the guests, confused and embarrassed, were starting to trickle out. The hotel manager and his assistant stood quietly to the side, bearing a cream envelope detailing the night's entertainment costs. The groom walked over to them and spread his hands, his mouth open, but no words came out.

The next day, the headline appeared in the tabloids, "ANG POWS STOLEN: WEDDING RUINED!"

෨ඵ

Kenny never knew exactly why he did it. The moment he saw the large red money box sitting by itself at the empty table, his first instinct was that *somebody should take it*. And out of self-preservation, he snagged it and ran.

The couple eventually paid for the wedding banquet by appealing to several relatives and by using "Kenny's money". Jonathan annulled the wedding and returned to New Jersey. Margaret decided to stay on in Singapore and ended up dating a Mr. Venantius Ong (whose real name was Boon Teck) from her church, whom Kenny thought she thoroughly deserved. Kenny applied to his American college, told his mother he won a full financial aid package, and went to Los Angeles with Chee Beng.

"I knew she was going to use my money," said Kenny. They were having dinner at a taco joint near campus. "I was in charge of calculating the wedding costs, and I knew she had it wrong. She was going to make a 30% loss, and she was going to use my money to plug the gap. By taking the red packets I actually doubled the money I had for my education."

He sketched out the figures on a paper napkin and showed the equation to Chee Beng.

"You know what, Kenny," said Chee Beng, looking down at the napkin and shaking his head. "You have got the *balls*."

And he was free to say it as loud as he liked, because nobody would report them.

THOSE WHO SERVE; THOSE WHO DO NOT

PETER WAS EIGHTEEN AND drove a truck for the Singapore Army. Joanne used to babysit him. They had a big family and the elder cousins would double up as babysitters. Peter was always sick as a dog back then. He almost didn't make it as a baby. Now he was a grown man and there he sat, on a hot August afternoon, smoking with his Army friends outside his flat, polishing his military boots and joking about girls.

"How's Army life?" Joanne asked, trying to connect with the mystery that Singaporean women had never been a part of. National Service was the male equivalent of having one's period—predestined to occur at a certain age, repeated throughout the most productive years of one's life, and entirely and relentlessly gender-specific. Like menstruation, it was an inscrutable rite of passage about which one gender hardly shared notes with the other. Still, it didn't keep Joanne from trying. "Is it horrible? Can you stand it?"

"So-so-*lah*! No time to see girlfriend!"

Joanne smiled. "And why haven't they shaved your head? I thought all Army guys have spiky short hair? Durian-heads?"

Peter chuckled, all ninety-eight pounds of him.

"Nowadays they are not so strict-*lah*!" Apparently Joanne had not kept in touch with the new face of the Singapore Army; her references were obsolete.

"How is your girlfriend taking your absence?"

Her cousin simply grinned. He was very shy around Joanne as she had lived abroad for some amount of time and he didn't remember her before she left Singapore.

Joanne, on the other hand, remembered the day Peter was born. She was in Primary Three. He weighed eight pounds, five ounces and had hair that stuck straight up. The other kids in the family called him "Elvis." Joanne helped her aunt to watch him after school, doing her homework with one hand and tugging at his sarong cradle with the other, until he fell asleep. Peter was plagued by coughs when he was growing up. They tried everything. Western doctors, Chinese doctors, home remedies, new types of milk formula. His mother even tried consulting a temple medium. Poor Peter was so overly medicated as a child that he was forever after underweight and "under tall".

Now he was five feet two of pure tanned leather, made sinewy by National Service. Still, he was considered by the Army to be too thin. To the envy of his friends, he was assigned to be a truck driver. He spent most of his time in National Service criss-crossing the island, shuttling troops back and forth between camps.

"Hey, you know what I found that is really cool?" Peter said, all of a sudden. "His friends stopped chattering for a bit and leaned forward. He slid his hand into his pocket and removed a dog-eared photograph.

"Tah-dah!"

It was a black-and-white photograph of his father Sam, Joanne's uncle. "This is my Lao Ba. My Dad!" said Peter, flashing it around like a collector's item. The picture said "Kuala Lumpur, 1973" at the back, and Private Samuel K.S. Goh was posing in his army gear on one of his first "overseas assignments".

"Da Tou Bing!" said Peter proudly. "Big-headed soldier" was what the Chinese in Singapore would exclaim whenever they see pictures of the Queen of England's guards marching in their tall black bearskins. In the photograph, Sam wore a huge British Issue helmet, so large that it slid forward and threatened to obscure his eyes and nose.

With sudden tenderness for the boy in the photograph, Peter said, "When I went for NS, I took this with me. I still keep it with me every day. I tell myself, NS can't be that bad, Lao Ba did it!"

Presently, Lao Ba himself came out into the sunlight from the dim recesses of the flat. Father and son were carbon copies of each other.

108

Peter began to negotiate with his father over the use of Sam's decrepit Toyota in the evening. His friends looked on with plaintive expressions; they needed it to drive to an all-important soccer game. It was their day off from the Army, and Peter was the only one with access to a car.

Joanne told Sam that Peter was exhibiting a picture of him from his Army days. Everyone laughed as her uncle feigned shock.

"Let me see!" he commanded, stretching out his open palm. "Where did you dig that up?"

"Mum found it! She said I could have it!" said Peter gleefully.

Joanne could tell that beneath Sam's indignation he was secretly pleased, in the typical Chinese father kind of way. He scrutinized the picture while the boys giggled.

"You guys don't know what it was like in those days!" said Sam. "Everything we used was what the British left behind. Huge helmets! Huge boots! All the stuff they didn't want after World War II, we ended up using them!"

Protestations of disbelief.

"World War II!" said Ravi, one of the boys. "Yeah, right!" Sam grew stern. "Hey Ravi, let me tell you, you guys are lucky. What is Army standard issue these days? Nike boots? They even have Velcro! And your backpack, looks like a Nike backpack, so high-tech. Looks like the kind I would pay money to buy in a sports shop. Your helmet, what is it made of these days? Super light titanium?"

The five boys roared with laughter, shaking their heads.

"Back in my day, I had to stuff my boots with newspaper! You were lucky to get something that is not three sizes too big. Back then, we didn't have this type of custom-made stuff. Singapore Army is rich now, you know. Your weapons look like those in The Matrix!"

The boys traded banter with Sam for a bit, comparing Army experiences and slagging off their Army sergeants. A lot of it was standard bathroom humor. But soon the boys grew restless; they were missing their soccer game. Sam grumbled and relinquished the car keys and the boys sped off, their voices echoing down the bright stairwell of the HDB block.

The lights were just popping up in the dusk, across thousands of households in the estate. Families were turning to blue flickering screens for dinner television.

"So how's life in Australia?" asked Sam, lighting a cigarette. Peter learned to smoke from him. They even held the cigarette to their mouths in the same way. Joanne felt a pang of envy. She never had that kind of rapport with her parents.

"Oh, it's OK, I guess."

"How's your mum?"

She looked over the inky-blueness of Singapore in the twilight. Thousands of orange-white dots blinked in the endless kingdoms of HDB flats that stretched as far as the eye could see. Tiny people leading tidy little capsuled lives. Somewhere, in Australia, Joanne's parents had a house with twelve times the square footage of an average HDB flat.

"She's fine. We don't talk much these days. She's on the west coast and Robert and I moved to the east when we got married."

"I keep forgetting Australia is a damn big place," her uncle grunted. He had never been there. "So what's keeping her busy?"

"She goes to church. Meets other Singaporeans that way."

"Hmph. I suppose it can get pretty lonely."

"Well, Perth has loads of ex-Singaporeans."

They listened to children laughing and tumbling about in the playground downstairs. The Malay "aunty" who lived next door returned from the market with some groceries for dinner. She nodded at them as she filed past, two children in tow.

Like many well-heeled Singaporeans, Joanne's parents had emigrated ten years ago because of her brother, Eddie. They didn't want Eddie to be enlisted for National Service when he turned eighteen. Because of mandatory conscription, one branch of Joanne's extended family voluntarily lopped itself off and transplanted itself on foreign soil. The wounds never healed.

"Haven't seen your brother in ten years. How is he?" asked her uncle. "Must be quite tall now, eh?"

She shrugged.

"Is it really true that he cannot come back?"

Yes, it was really true. Male children were not allowed to travel overseas for an extended period of time without their parents having posted a bond to ensure their return for mandatory conscription. Her parents took Eddie out of Singapore without paying this sum of money. It was a prohibitively large sum, designed to deter "leavers."

"If Eddie comes back for a visit, they think that the airport authorities would not let him out of Singapore again," she said. "They might impose the bond payment, or make him serve NS immediately."

Her uncle nodded. She knew, that he knew this was the reason. But he was hoping that one day he will get a different answer out of her. Each time she returned to Singapore for a visit, he asked the same question. All her uncles did. They didn't have money for casual trips to Australia, and her parents were too busy with their new life to visit. Over time, Joanne was the only one who ever made the trip back to Singapore to see the extended family.

She tried to console her uncle.

"Eddie is quite happy. He doesn't remember Singapore much. He's quite Australian these days; got it from his boarding school. He plays rugby now."

"Your dad plays with him?"

Joanne laughed. "Oh, no. You know what he's like. Always flying here and there on business trips." Even if her father smoked, Eddie would never learn to hold cigarettes the same way.

Sam added, matter-of-factly, "Your grandpa and grandma really miss Eddie. Your grandma says she dreams of Eddie sometimes."

Like all of Joanne's uncles, he had a genteel nature that did not openly disapprove. For all his protestations, he knew that her parents, like Chinese emigrants throughout the centuries, had performed a cost-benefit analysis. He knew that the costs were tremendous. And yet —"Hey, I was reading in the papers the other day," began Sam hopefully, "you know that world famous violin prodigy, Emanuel Seah? His parents took him away from Singapore when he was little and he grew up in London? He told a Singaporean reporter that he was scared of National Service and he refused to come back here to perform. The next day, the government said it was OK for him to come back. No bond payment, no penalty, no NS. Some MINDEF spokeswoman came straight out and declared it to the newspaper."

Joanne laughed. From time to time, her uncles would write or call her with such stories. Apparently, the hand of the State lifted to receive and forgive the sports gold medalists, the child piano prodigies. The policy would be revoked for the gifted few; the authorities were not inflexible. She had a feeling that her passionate uncles actually combed tabloids for such examples, so that Eddie could come back.

"So? Did the violinist come back?"

"Don't know-*lah*!" shrugged Sam. Sam never finished his secondary school education; the irony of special exemptions for the rich and the talented was lost on him. He didn't mind if his nephew, born into a wealthier generation, profited from it. Sam's mother was a hawker, his father drove a taxi cab by day and doubled as a racehorse-betting "bookie" by night. They were too poor even to let him and his brothers complete school. They certainly didn't have money to whisk them away to grow up in Australia, Canada, or any of those exotic emigrant havens where thousands of Singaporean boys now hid.

"Can waive NS like that, not bad right?" grinned Sam impishly. "Lucky bastard." He was genuinely happy that someone could get away scot-free from National Service. Others might have been tempted to write protracted complaints to the press on this issue. Still others, like Joanne's parents, could pontificate loudly on Singapore's "unjust" National Service policy during rounds of golf with their friends at the country club (they especially disliked posting the bond—why, you could get a lesser club membership for that money!). But not Sam. There was no bitterness there.

Joanne had always marveled at her uncle's stoicism, his easy co-existence with the natural inequities of life on one hand, and the unfairness of government policy on the other. That eternal torch of optimism. Her university-bred self could never tolerate it. She looked at the thousands of HDB homes that fanned out from either side of Sam's tiny flat. Did each of these modest little homes contain people like Sam? Or was he a dying breed? She suddenly felt her heart open. These were the people who will protect the country, she thought. Thousands and thousands of nameless, faceless, sun-darkened, sinewy men like Sam and his son Peter and their friends, who smoked, played soccer, and reported dutifully every year for their reservist training, simply because that was what was on the cards for them. They could not afford arrogance or fancy arguments. Against such a solid breakwater the waves of cynicism would crash, but would fail. When the time came, it would be precisely this nature on which courage would be founded.

"Is Eddie still as fat? He used to be *sooo* fat when he was a baby, remember? And my Peter was *sooo* skinny. We used to call them Laurel and Hardy. *Ah Pui* and *Ah Sang*," Sam reminisced.

"He's not fat anymore. He's taller than me now."

Her uncle blew the smoke out in grey-blue rings into the dusk. For a long time, neither spoke.

Then Sam said, "Actually, NS isn't really that bad. All of us—Uncle Bobby, Uncle Chris, Uncle Jerry – served NS. We survived, didn't we?"

"I know." said Joanne. She adds, "But then again, I'm a girl."

They both laughed.

She was grateful that her uncle left the discussion at that. He continued to smoke quietly, looking out at the darkening blue distance, until her aunt called them both in for dinner.

THE SHOOTING RANCH

I. GRACE

WHEN AUNTY LILLIAN FROM Singapore heard that I would be in Las Vegas, she asked if I could visit her daughter. Grace lived in Nevada.

"You have a daughter who lives in Nevada?" I asked, surprised.

"Oh yes, yes. On a farm."

A farm? In the desert? What kind of Singaporean would do that? I imagined a bronzed, beefy type with a loud laugh. Sun-streaked hair, athletic limbs. Taming cows. Raising pigs. *Livin' La Vida Loca.*

Imagine my disappointment when Grace turned out to be a tiny Chinese woman with bluish-ivory skin and large, bulging eyes. She had a heart-shaped face framed by scalloped curls. She looked like those ladies in Chinese women's fashion magazines—back in 1973. I'll never forget what she was wearing that day. A plain white cotton smock— the kind of thing you would sew in a Home Economics class as an introduction to dress-making. It was austere, almost Amish.

"Mom," whined my daughter Anouk behind me. Anouk was reaching that age where girls would commit suicide if they didn't wear the right cut of jeans. She already had reservations about Grace Lee. During the drive I had mentioned that Grace met her husband through a church pen pal network. She was in Singapore; he was studying in the United States. They wrote letters, fell in love long-distance, she came over to meet and marry him. My daughter thought it was so uncool. Love, she thought, was like one of those E.M. Forster Italian novels. You run into a handsome stranger in Florence, he sweeps you off your feet, your life is changed forever. I had a gay British novelist to thank for putting thoughts of impossible heterosexual bliss into my twelve-year-

114

old's head. "A church pen-pal network?" she had asked incredulously. Anouk now contemplated Grace like she was some kind of insect.

"Hi, Grace," I gave her a hug.

Grace was in a daze. She said she was not used to having visitors. "I can't believe my mother asked you to come see me! So embarrassing. I can't believe you drove all this way. My mother is always thinking of me in Singapore. How was the drive?" Grace might have left our country many years ago, but her accent was as firm and crisp as if she had just been plucked out of a Singapore housing estate by an alien spacecraft and plonked right in the middle of Nevada.

"This is my daughter, Anouk." I said. I gave Anouk a look. She had not wanted to be driven three hundred miles across the desert to be here.

Grace was confused by the name. "Ah Look? Ah Nook?"

Anouk, who at age six taught herself French and German, wore black turtlenecks, and would smoke gauloises if I let her, broke out into a cold sweat at finding herself suddenly among the Uncool. I propelled her cheerfully towards the house, chatting with Grace with as much gaiety as I could muster.

"So, let's take a look at your digs. Is this a real farm?"

"Well, um, yes, oh, used to be. Come inside! Come inside! It's so cold today!" She laughed nervously and folded her arms across her tiny breasts beneath the thin cotton dress.

We began walking up the dirt track towards a wooden house painted a dirty yellow. It had a flat roof of slate tiles and peeling whitewashed posts on the front verandah. It looked like it had been built in several phases. An extra bedroom stuck out brutally on the left side, and a new bathroom, on the right. The building looked like it had been put together with some tools and materials from Home Depot for $149.99. Richard Meier was not at work here.

I felt sad all of a sudden. Grace's parents lived in a small government-subsidized flat in Singapore, but at least it had the feel of a solid bourgeois existence, like most Singaporean homes. Aunty Lillian told me that Grace and her husband didn't have much money out here in

Nevada, but there was nothing more depressing than rural poverty in temperate climates. Sure, you had a big house, which gave you more square footage than any Singaporean could afford. But it was only an illusion of wealth and plenty. A closer look, and the house would just be made of wood, not bricks, and the inside would usually be lined with industrial carpeting and other flimsy flammable materials. Sure, you had a car, but it would be a beaten-up station wagon, not a shiny little bug of a Toyota that most Singaporeans aspired towards. And, unlike most Singaporeans, you had a yard, but it would just be Nevada desert scrub on which nobody would put a price tag. Life was cheap in America.

"Anouk really loves animals," I said, giving her a glare. Break the ice, everybody!

"Really? Oh dear." said Grace.

"Are there any cows or horses or dogs?" I asked.

"Um. No." Grace ushered us into a drippy-looking mud room with boots and tools. It smelled musty, as if no one had lived there for years. "Melissa! Mindy! Come and call Aunty."

Anouk was giving me the look of death. *There are no animals, so what kind of farm is that? You know I like animals. You blew it Mom!*

I stuck my tongue out at her and she stuck it back when Grace was not looking. "So," I said, "your girls must be around Anouk's age."

"How old is Ah Look?" said Grace admiringly, looking her up and down.

"Twelve." said Anouk.

"Wah! But she she's so big! I thought she is sixteen. She looks so matured. My twins are fourteen, but they are so much shorter!"

Anouk looked at me, I could hear her mentally voicing in anguish, *"Mature-d?"*

Two little girls came down the rickety stairs slowly. They wore their hair in neat braids. They were dressed alike in thin cotton pajamas with long sleeves and trousers that appeared to be made from the same bolt of cloth as Grace's outfit. I looked around the parlor, and sure enough, there was a sewing machine in a yellowing plastic case. Hadn't seen those in a while. I didn't think anyone back in New York owned a sewing machine, unless they were in the fashion industry or worked in a sweatshop.

The parlor exuded a forlorn air. From the ceiling, a crooked plastic lamp hung half-heartedly. Through the plastic bowl cover of the lamp, I could see the dark shadows of dead little moths that had flown into the lamp from summers past. The walls were colored industrial gray, the wall-to-wall acrylic carpet a flocked salt-and-pepper. The curtains were hand-sewn and made of a kind of nondescript polyester floral fabric — the kind that you would find in Quality Inns and Motel 6's. In the center of the parlor was an immense old-fashioned black stove. It was the only source of heat in this dusty, cluttered parlor.

"It burns real wood," noted Anouk with awe. She held her hands out to it, sensing the live fire within. Before, she thought heat came from a socket in the wall.

The parlor led into an eat-in kitchen. Mismatched dining chairs made out of rust-speckled chrome and "pleather." A formica-topped dining table with a faulty leg. A plywood shelf with some knick-knacks. A framed cross-stitch sampler which said, in pink and blue Gothic lettering, *The Lord Is My Shepherd*. It was all very noir, very depressing, particularly because everything was old without being historic or quaint. Modern stuff, just aged. They had every American convenience — a large refrigerator, dishwasher, toaster, oven, four-ring gas stove. You had a feeling that these guys never ate out. Maybe there wasn't anywhere to eat out at — there was nothing in the town that we drove through that exuded civilization, except for the large gas station and the convenience store attached to it.

"Would you like some cheesecake? I made it myself." said Grace. Immediately Anouk and I brightened. Homemade cheesecake sounded great. Grace got out some orange plastic plates and we sat round the dining table, careful to avoid the faulty leg which, if bumped, sent everything on the table shivering.

"So, where's Henry? Does he know we are coming?" I asked.

Grace fussed around a Tupperware tub, dishing out big globs of a yellow substance.

"He works as a lab technician in the next town. It's a long drive, two hours. He gets home late. He knows, of course, that you are coming. Girls, do you want some?"

The twins shook their heads. Up till now they had not said a single word, just lounged shyly in their chairs. They were not identical twins. Melissa had big teeth and a boyish air. Mindy was tiny and feminine. She reminded me of a starving French actress in a film based on one of Marguerite Duras' books. *Hiroshima Mon Amour*, *The Lover*—she was gangly, with that lost look of someone trapped in a basement. Beside Anouk, the twins were so thin and stringy that they looked like they were made by a creator who ran out of raw material.

Grace made some instant coffee and we sat round eating her cheesecake. Grace and the twins didn't have any; they just watched us politely. I wondered if the twins were brought up under a famous Singaporean creed: "Children should be seen and not heard." They had not said a word to us. The smell of instant coffee brought back memories. My parents in Singapore used to make instant coffee—something that one ceased to have once coffee bars took over urban life. It was a familiar taste; I didn't dislike it, but Anouk was sipping it gingerly. It was all my husband's fault. He brought Anouk up into that worst of urban monsters, the coffee snob. *Please don't shame me*, I prayed.

The room was silent. Grace and her kids watched us with interest as we took each bite, as if we were celebrities. I half expected a camera flash to pop. I tried to be perky.

"So, how do you like your life here? I'm amazed that you bake. I can't really bake anything. Do you cook a lot?"

Grace looked confused through her glasses. "Oh, yes. I love to bake. How do you like the cake, Ah Look?"

"It's nice." said Anouk icily and prettily. Or maybe only I could detect the ice, because she seemed to reassure Grace, who beamed.

Grace asked after my husband.

"Oh, he's fine. He's attending a conference in Las Vegas today, so it's just as well we're out here with you. Anouk and I were getting bored with the casinos."

"He's *ang moh*, isn't he?"

"Yes, he's white." I braced myself for the usual interrogation. Chinese people could be so curious. No question was too private. People could straightforwardly ask you about your salary, your rent, your white husband. Of course, other things were never discussed: emotions, sex, the truth. But a white husband: well, that was up for grabs. That was a curiosity, a side show. People had the right to know.

"Quite a few Chinese girls now marry *ang mohs* these days. It's so common now." said Grace delicately. "How long have you been married?"

"Thirteen years."

"Wah." said Grace politely. "So, how you find him?" (She meant: "how do I like my husband"?)

"John's a great guy. I'm lucky to have met him." Thirteen years of shared existence, summed up in one tidy PR line. I changed the subject. "So, why does your mom and dad think you are living on a farm? There doesn't seem to be any animals out here."

"Oh, there's the woods." Grace gulped and gestured vaguely at the dusty window. "Behind. We keep animals."

"What kind of animals?" asked Anouk with interest.

"Pheasants." Grace looked helpless, as if surprised that we didn't understand. "It's a shooting range out back, people—tourists—come and hunt. We raise some pheasants and rabbits out there in cages. When the hunting season begins we collect money from people who let them loose in the woods to shoot them."

"Really. How nice," I said brightly, kicking Anouk under the table as she opened her mouth. Besides being a coffee snob, my daughter also had certain views about animal rights. It's not me, I swear, it's her school. That's how they are taught these days. Anouk was born, like Athena, with all of her full faculties and a PETA bumper sticker attached. I *was* appalled that Grace and Henry actually ran a shooting ranch, but I was doing this for Aunty Lillian who was seventy-six, and who was I to judge.

Melissa spoke for the first time.

"Sometimes Mindy and I go out and save the rabbits. There's always one or two who get wounded and forgotten by everybody and we take them home and nurse them."

"You know Daddy doesn't like that," said Grace. "Once they're sold to the hunters, it's not our property anymore."

"We can't leave them out to die," said Mindy softly.

My daughter looked at her with beseeching eyes, then at me.

"Mom, I need to go to the bathroom," she said in a strangled voice. She rose and wandered in the indicated direction. I hoped it was not to puke. Grace's cheesecake was exactly what she said it was—it tasted like all she did was pack Philly cream cheese straight into a tin and baked it. Her years in America did not teach her American cooking. I felt pretty sick myself.

"Is it too rich?" asked Grace anxiously. "Henry likes his cheesecake very rich."

"Oh no, it's lovely," I said. I darted a glance at my watch and counted the hours till we left the next day. Could I even last that long? I started to feel desperate. "So, what keeps you busy all day when Henry is away in the next town?"

Grace beamed at me through her glasses. "Oh, we can get quite busy. We do some work with the rabbit hutches, we feed the birds. There is some brush wood to gather for the iron stove. We only have electricity from a generator in the back, so we try to burn wood when we can. And anyway, I'm expecting."

"You are? Congratulations!" I said. The baby was due in the spring, and Henry was going to build a new nursery room out in the back. "Wow, what a life," I said. "Certainly very different from Singapore, huh? You're a regular Martha Stewart."

"Who?" asked Grace curiously.

"Oh, um. Just someone on TV, " I said quickly.

"Martha's the doyenne of home-making," announced Anouk, back from her bathroom trip. "Don't you watch her on TV?"

"We don't have TV," said Melissa. She had thick eyebrows that almost met in the middle, inherited perhaps from her father. She now drew them together in an intense frown.

Anouk looked as if she was going to have some kind of apoplectic fit.

"You don't have *television*?" The three girls looked at each other. I caught Grace's eye and winked. "Anouk's a bit of a *screenager*. You know, glued to screens. Computer screens, TV. Why don't you show us around your house?"

Grace blinked.

"Oh, sure. Sure. I'll show you your room. Actually, you have to share with the girls because we never thought of building a guest room. We never have guests. Usually. Ha ha. Come to the front."

We cleared our dishes and followed Grace and her kids down the corridor.

I recall reading that each year at the Cannes film festival they would screen a few American movies informally known as "the rurals" which were always about non-urban, non-East Coast American life in the latter half of the 20th century. Lots of movies fall into that category. *Jesus Son. My Own Private Idaho. Affliction. The Straight Story. Buffalo 66.* The rustic mid-West, or the South, or the other forgotten corners of the US of A would unfurl gorgeously on the big screen, full of disused gas stations, tumbleweed, roads that lead poker-straight into the horizon. Men would wear beaten up leather jackets and almost always some sort of hat, and the women would be raggedly blond and in some kind of trashy-pretty house dress that expensive women's clothing lines tried very hard to duplicate. Everyone would have some problem —violence, sex, drugs, poverty, incest, alcoholism, or just boredom.

It was strange to see Grace Lee, daughter of Aunty Lillian and Uncle Yew Hock (who ran a hawker stall in a food court), in the thick of this rusticity. Grace, who wore braids and went to the Convent of the Holy Infant Jesus in Singapore, who spoke with a thick Hokkien-inflected accent (still, after all those years). *Congratulations, Grace. You have been where no Singaporean has ever gone before. You were so brave to fall in love long-distance.* I looked at the interior of the house, which could have come out off the set of a Coen Brothers movie, and wondered again at the adaptability of Singaporeans. Sure, she couldn't bake, but it was utterly amazing that she could live here like this, so far away from the clean-scrubbed concrete public housing estates that she grew up in. I should stop congratulating myself about adjusting to life in New York. I was a wimp compared to Grace.

"Do you guys have CDs?" I heard Anouk asking the twins.

"No."

"What about a CD player?"

Melissa looked at Mindy, and they both giggled nervously.

"No." said Melissa. "Not if we don't have CDs."

"Are you sure you don't have TV?"

"Yes." said Mindy.

"Never had TV?"

"I saw some TV at school once," said Melissa. "About the life of insects. For science class."

"That doesn't count. I'm talking about HBO and Cinemax. *The Sopranos. Sex and the City.* Cable?"

Melissa giggled again.

"No. I mean, I know what cable is, but we don't have it."

Anouk was becoming a real interrogator, earnest and pleading.

"Do you have the Internet?"

"No." said Mindy and Melissa together.

"You don't even have the Internet? You've got to be fucking kidding me!"

I turned round and flashed her with my eyes.

"Sorry, I didn't mean to say fucking. But Mom, did you—"

"Yes. I heard. Anouk, you're on a farm. There are no fiber optic cables out here."

Melissa shrugged.

"I think we can get it. But our dad won't let us have it." Mindy chimed in, "He says if we watch TV or go on the Internet we'll forget about school."

Grace agreed heartily. "Yes, yes. I agree. We are very strict. You let Ah Look watch TV?"

I laughed. "I don't know if I *let* her do it, or it just exists. Like oxygen. Do I let her breathe? I guess."

II. HENRY

Grace had laid the table for dinner. On one side of the rickety table there was a plate of hamburgers (already in their buns), peas and mashed potatoes. On the other, a pot of white jasmine rice, stir-fried celery, carrots and straw mushrooms, and a bowl of hot pork rib soup.

Anouk and I had spent the latter part of the day with the twins out in the woods while Grace was making dinner. We perused the rabbit hutches, and for the pheasant cages, we had to put on brightly-colored hunting vests to explore the woods, which was just a few acres of scrubby wintry wasteland. The twins seemed much happier out in there. They knew the names of the trees and the grasses, and showed us an old Balboa tree. Anouk brought a camera so she took a picture of the tree, misshapen and demonic against the gathering purple–black dusk.

"Mom, the girls asked me if I was Asian." whispered Anouk as we walked back towards the house. The twins were lagging behind, picking up sticks for firewood.

"So?"

"I said I was half-Asian and half-white. They said I didn't look Asian."

"Well, honey, it is what it is. You gotta tell her you're my daughter and if I'm Chinese that means you're half. Unless your dad got you from a test tube."

"Mom, I'm serious. They were kinda weird about it."

"Look, I think you've established by now that these guys don't really seem to know anybody out here in the sticks. So the concept of a biracial marriage is probably out of their—you know—range. So they're not going to be very PC about things. You're not in Kansas anymore."

"What do you mean? I am *totally* in Kansas, sort of. The sticks."

"Honey, it's a famous line not to be taken literally."

"What does it mean to look Asian anyway," began Anouk crossly. "I'm not Asian. I'm part-Chinese and part-French-Polish-Czech. Asian doesn't mean anything."

"Sure it does. In America, Asian means we're the kind of people who live in between the covers of books with geishas pictured on the front and titles written in brushstroke font. Usually a bird or flower forms part of the title. *Memories of Lotus Leaves. Grandmother's Peony Diaries. Palace Dreams and Wild Cranes. My Hurting Achy Bound Feet.* That kind of thing."

Anouk was laughing helplessly when we entered the house.

"My, what a spread!" I exclaimed at the sight of the dinner table.

"I hope you like this? I think you take Western food? I got some specially from the supermarket for you," Grace said eagerly,

"Oh Grace, as I said on the phone, we really eat anything." I was starting to feel bad. "You needn't cook special meals for us. We eat Chinese all the time."

"What about Ah Look? She's half *ang moh*, she must only like hamburgers, right?" fussed Grace. "Sit, sit."

Anouk actually disliked hamburgers and constantly railed at John and me for eating at McDonald's. Something about a book she read about the American beef industry. Thankfully, she was concentrating too much on avoiding the hamburgers to pick a fight about being identified by Grace as "half *ang moh*".

"Oops, here comes Henry," said Grace brightly, as if she tripped over something.

The torn screen door slammed and a short little Chinese man came in. He was much older than I had expected. Henry had graying wiry hair and a very tanned, compact little body, and looked kind of like a wombat. As I had guessed, he was the one with the Unibrow. It gave him an odd, angry look. He had huge glasses with yellowing plastic frames that covered almost half his face, like those of the geeks in *Weird Science*. No wonder he worked in a lab. He wore polyester grey pants (the crinkle-free type), and a polo shirt under his winter jacket. The polo shirt said "Arnold Palmer" in curlicues and had a little umbrella embroidered on the breast pocket. He looked like an irritable little Japanese tourist who had strayed off from his golf package tour and ended up here on this shooting ranch by mistake. Like Grace, he wore a silver cross which gleamed against his dark skin.

"Dinner ready already?" he said to no one in particular.

"Henry, this is Sarah and Ah Look." said Grace brightly, gesturing towards us.

"Huh?" he grunted. He was so like my father, I thought all of a sudden. Every inch of him oozed Chinese male patriarch. My father used to grunt like that at guests, because he didn't really know how to grasp the idea that someone was visiting him.

"Hi Henry, I'm Sarah." I reached to shake his hand. He refused to take it and just nodded at me, as if I was a young girl and he did not shake hands with children.

"Where's my pork soup?" Henry had a quintessential Singaporean accent as well. It was rather odd to hear that in the middle of a Coen Brothers film set.

"And this is Anouk, my daughter," I said. Henry nodded at her and sat himself down. I heard him mutter under his breath, "Five women! Eating dinner with five women! It is bad enough as it is with three, day in, day out."

"Well, I guess we can all start." said Grace, busying herself. "Henry doesn't like to wait, he's always starving after the long drive."

"Who said I'm starving?" demanded Henry, not looking at his wife. "Where's my chopsticks?"

"Here."

"Eat, eat," said Henry brusquely, waving at all of us.

I guessed that was a sign to begin. Anouk and I were reaching for the hamburgers when we stopped short. The Lee family had bowed their head in prayer. We waited, a little ill at ease. Anouk looked at me and rolled her eyes.

"OK, eat eat." said Henry. "No need to stand on ceremony. We don't stand on ceremony in this house. Eat!"

The Lee family didn't really believe in conversation. He was a real charmer, that one.

125

We ate for some time in awful silence. Grace kept looking at her husband, at Melissa, at Mindy, then at us nervously. Anouk and I tried to pretend we loved hamburgers.

"Why cook this sort of thing?" demanded Henry all of a sudden, gesturing at the mashed potatoes.

"Oh, I thought I would make Western food for Sarah and her daughter."

"Oh? You don't take Chinese?" Henry turned to me, his face twisted into a sudden sneer. "You not Chinese meh?"

"I am, in fact. I told Grace we eat Chinese, but it was very nice of her to try to make something special." I said firmly.

"Your daughter does not look Chinese. Are you sure you are Chinese?"

I said I was from Singapore like him and Grace.

"Really?" Henry's voice rose. He looked at me with unadulterated contempt. I remembered something my dad used to say. *No one can hate a Singaporean so much as another Singaporean.* I used to think my dad was deliberately being cynical, but suddenly I got a whiff of what he meant.

He continued, "How come you don't sound Singaporean? Huh? You don't even act Singaporean."

"I've lived in the States for a long time." I still hoped I sounded friendly and firm, although I could see Anouk had this Joan of Arc look in her eyes and half expected her to go flying at him any moment.

He continued his interrogation, challenging me, baiting me, trying to sound me out for being a phoney. He wanted me to prove that deep down, I was just like him. He didn't want me to put on airs and eat hamburgers in his house. He seemed to have problems with Chinese women who did not kowtow to him, like Grace and his daughters did. It was some type of arcane contest, like two cats watching each other warily, hackles up, until one backed down. I wasn't going to back down. I felt sad all of a sudden. Would people of other nationalities do this upon meeting a compatriot? What was it about Singaporeans, I wondered dimly, as he continued his taunts.

"You Hokkien or what?" He spoke with his mouth full, and a grain of rice flew from his lips and landed on the tabletop.

"Cantonese, actually."

"Oh." He laughed. "So you understand the word, *guai mui*?"

I smiled blankly. "Sure."

He turned to Anouk. "You know, girl, *guai mui*? You know what that means?"

"No." said Anouk dangerously. Her eyes glittered. I came to her rescue.

"Uncle Henry is trying to say the word for Caucasian women. I think he thinks that we are not Chinese enough."

Henry laughed again, his chopsticks in his left hand, his rice bowl in his right. He looked at his wife, sharing the joke.

"Grace, *guai mui*, explain it to the little girl. It's not Caucasian woman. It's devil woman!"

"Very nice." I said cheerfully. "Anouk and I are definitely devil women, aren't we, Anouk?"

"So your daughter here is a *pak zheng-lah*?"

I knew that word too. It was the word in the *Hokkien* dialect for mixed race. Actually, it sounded more like a veterinary term and literally meant to inject (an animal) with genes for a desired breed. I was Singaporean enough to know that even in Singapore people did not use that word on people of mixed races. Maybe only behind their backs.

"What's that, Mom?" asked Anouk sullenly, fixing her famous stare on Henry.

"Oh, I think Uncle Henry wants to know if you are half-Chinese and half-white. Which she is." I said, turning to Henry. "I really must compliment you on your wife's cooking."

"You like it, tell her so. You must be the only one! Huh!" grunted Henry with another sneer and slurped his soup loudly, directly from his bowl. "Melissa, more rice!"

Melissa, who had eaten hardly anything since the meal began, got up and took his rice bowl from him. She walked round the table and filled it for him from the pot.

"You marry *ang moh*, this is what you get." said Henry all of a sudden, to no one in particular. Then, he humphed to himself, as if sharing a private sneer with God. "Grace here, she thought she was going to marry an *ang moh*. Didn't you, Grace?"

"Nonsense, dear." said Grace, forcing another hamburger on Anouk.

"Why don't you just come out and admit it. You wrote me those letters back then, thinking you were going to marry an American. You didn't know Henry Lee was a Chinese man. A Chinaman."

"I don't know what he's talking about!" laughed Grace. "Of course I knew you were a Singaporean."

"Yah right." said Henry. "More soup! So, Sarah. You did better than Grace. She must admire you very much. She likes the *ang mohs*. Every single bloody day she wants to leave this house and go out there and talk to our *ang moh* neighbors. What's there to talk about! They come here, we take their money, they shoot our birds, end of story. Fair and square."

"We have very nice neighbors down the road." said Grace, attempting to explain to me, although I wasn't interested in anything by now except hoping that her husband would choke on a pork rib, keel over and die. "Mr and Mrs McGrady. Retired couple. Mrs McGrady is going to teach me how to make an apple pie with Ritz crackers and applesauce."

"Pie pie pie. You and your stupid cakes and pies. That's not Chinese food. *Ang moh* food is not welcome in my house." said Henry. He turned on Mindy suddenly. "Are you wearing lipstick?"

"No." said Mindy. The little color on her face drained very quickly.

He stuck his dark face very close to hers, scrutinizing her lips intensely. "Are you sure? Why are your lips so red?" He breathed heavily on her and her bangs fluttered.

"I don't own any lipstick, Dad."

"Maybe you got it from your mother?"

Mindy looked at her mother, quivering. Her twin sat frozen in her seat.

"Dear, she is not wearing any lipstick, don't imagine things." said Grace. "It's cold today, she's just flushed."

"If I catch her wearing any makeup I'll give her two tight slaps." Henry burped and shoved rice into his mouth with his chopsticks. He said, muffled through his food, "I work hard, for what? To raise a household of sluts."

Under the table, I found Anouk's very cold hand, balled into a fist, and gave it what I hoped to be a comforting squeeze.

III. THE TWINS

Twelve hours. Twelve hours were all you needed to understand a family: peel back its layers, one by one. From utter strangers we became co-conspirators. Or so it felt that night when we went to bed.

I slept on a pull-out mattress in the twins' room. Anouk piled into the bed with the twins. It was very cold in the room. Desert temperatures could drop below fifty degrees, and it always seemed so much colder indoors than outdoors. The polyester-stuffed duvet that was given to me afforded little warmth.

"I like your alarm clock." said Anouk to the twins. I pretended to be asleep, but the night light was on and I could see the girls talking to each other. Anouk was whispering.

"Thanks." Melissa whispered back. "It was a birthday present from my mom."

There was a long silence.

"Actually, my dad doesn't know this, but it has a radio function as well. Sometimes when he is out, Mom, Mindy and I tune in to listen to music."

"Really."

"Yeah. Aside from this radio alarm clock, nothing else in this house really produces any music." said Mindy.

"That sucks. So what kind of music do you listen to?"

"Anything, as long as we can get good reception," said Melissa. There was long sigh in the darkness. "Country, rock, jazz. Even the DJ's voice, and the commercials. It sounds so comforting. To know that on 555 Western Avenue there is a big sale going on, all furniture must go. That they are expecting airport delays due to a snowstorm in Denver. That sort of thing."

Mindy added, "We have to be careful though, because if Dad hears us listening to radio he would get really mad."

"What's his problem?" asked Anouk.

Silence. Then—"We don't know. Mom says he just doesn't want us to grow up into bad kids." said Melissa.

"He thinks TV and radio and all that makes you turn bad." said Mindy.

"Define bad."

The twins were silent.

"That really sucks, it's like you are permanently grounded." concluded Anouk.

"Yeah." said one twin.

"Grounded for life." Added the other.

"Do you like your school?"

"Yeah. I like being with people." said Melissa.

Mindy added, "Although they think we're weird because we don't have TV And they hate our clothes. It's worse because we're twins and we dress the exact same way in these clothes. They pick on us like crazy."

"Your clothes are fine."

"Dad doesn't allow us to wear skirts. Mom makes all our clothes." said Mindy.

Anouk gasped. "You've got to be fucking kidding me."

"Dad says skirts are for sluts. He doesn't allow us to buy clothes from the mall." said Mindy. "He says they are too revealing."

"Gawd. Is your dad some kind of religious freak?"

"I never thought about that. He's from Singapore." said Mindy.

Silence. Then Melissa said, "Is your mom sleeping?"

"I guess she is."

"I like your mom."

"Thanks. She's all right."

"Before I met her today I thought all Singaporeans were like my dad and mom."

"Well, how many have you met?"

"None, really. We never met our grandparents. We get letters from them sometimes, money in red packets, but Dad keeps them. I don't know what they say in those letters. My dad doesn't like my mom's parents. And he's stopped talking to his family many years ago." said Melissa.

"Your Dad doesn't like anybody." said Anouk.

"What's Singapore like? Is everyone like my dad?" said Mindy.

"No fucking way. They have Tower Records. And first-run Hollywood movies. And Lasertag."

"Then how come my mom and dad are like that?" said Mindy.

"Don't know. Maybe some Singaporeans are like that. Or maybe they come out here and turn bad."

"Oh." Mindy sighed. "Maybe some day we'll go visit Singapore."

"I hope you do."

"Maybe we can go together?" said Melissa.

Anouk wriggled around in the bed for warmth. "You bet, that's a pact. You wouldn't want to come back here. This place stinks. Your mom should totally divorce your dad."

Melissa said, "Once, when he hit us, Mom said she was going for a divorce."

Anouk drew her breath in sharply.

"Well, she's been saying that for years, especially whenever he hits us. He hits her all the time. He only hits us on our body, not on our arms and legs. He doesn't want our teachers to see the marks." I heard a rustle as Melissa pulled up her nightgown and showed Anouk something. "Mindy, show Anouk."

"Don't want to," said Mindy in a stubborn, small voice.

Anouk said, her voice louder, "Why don't you call the cops!"

"Mom doesn't let us. She says that we should never get the Americans involved in our household affairs." said Melissa.

Her twin added, "She says the Americans look down on us enough as it is, and they won't help us. We're just Chinese immigrants. Mom says she doesn't know enough about the laws here and she's afraid."

"I'd call the cops." said Anouk resolutely. "Especially if my dad was beating me."

"I'm not afraid of my Dad beating me," said Melissa. "What I mind is how he stops me from talking to other people. Girls and boys. And how he won't let us have any contact with our neighbors, because he is paranoid about people reporting him to the police. He's afraid of white people. I guess he got treated badly by some white guys once when he was in school, and he hates the white people that he works with at the lab."

Mindy added promptly, "He says they look down on him."

"Would he talk to Chinese people?"

The twins conferred with each other, then Mindy said, "Only if they are from Singapore, but there aren't many of them in this part of Nevada. Dad hates people from mainland China, and he looks down on Taiwanese and Vietnamese immigrants. He says people from Singapore are better than those people and that we have nothing in common with them."

"Jeez." Anouk considered the question at hand. "Why don't you guys run away from him? Pile into the car and drive off?"

"We can't," said Mindy. "He is the only one allowed to use the car. He hides the keys at night. Anyway, my mom's afraid of pulling a stunt like that."

"Anyway, where are we going to go?" said Melissa. "We don't have any relatives in America."

"Can't your mom think of something?" Anouk was desperate. In her world there were no unsolvable problems. She always had spunk. Already in her head she was devising all kinds of escape plans suitable for spunky kids that would make Steven Spielberg proud. I could hear the cogs and wheels whirring.

"She's afraid of my dad," said Melissa. "And anyway, it's been so many years. I think she loves him still. We were hoping she would go through with the divorce with some money she saved, but last week she told us she was going to spend it on the nursery room for the new baby. I think she changed her mind ever since she got pregnant."

A silence ensued, where the three girls lay side by side, contemplating the awfulness of humanity. Evil seemed to stretch on and on to eternity—banal, simple, unexpected evil.

For a while I felt Anouk's indignation. Then common sense flooded in. It's too dramatic to call this evil, I thought suddenly. This was a familiar story. These were shards of somebody else's married life, tossed up for our temporary contemplation, like garbage bobbing on the sea that we looked at idly from the prow of a luxury cruise ship. *We're just passing through, Anouk. We can't do anything. This is the detritus of someone else's marriage.*

But I could hear her heart thumping with the savage indignation of a child. For a long time, Melissa's words held us all in an awful web in the cold silence. Outside, in the still desert night, the insect noises ebbed and flowed like dry waves in the dark.

IV. DO SOMETHING

We were speeding in the white Ford Explorer into the morning sun.

I was lost in my own thoughts. Anouk was not her chirpy self. She played with the radio.

"The mayor has said today that he expects a settlement to be reached with the union very soon. And now, for sports. After blowing a seven-run lead the previous night that led to a disappointing home loss, the 51s were faced with the possibility that if they didn't beat the Edmonton Trappers Thursday night, their first-round playoff series could be over in a hurry . . ."

That morning, Anouk had spent some time with the twins in their hunting vests in the woods again, while Grace packed some extra cheesecake in a Tupperware container for me. We exchanged some low-level pleasantries. Neither of us talked about her husband, who had already left before we woke up.

"I've really got to go, Grace, we have a long drive ahead." I rose to call the kids.

Grace followed me out into the sunlight with her Tupperware box and I put our things into the car.

"Thanks so much for letting us stay with you. And for making dinner and breakfast."

"Oh, my pleasure, my pleasure."

"Good luck with the baby." I gave her a hug. "I'll let your mom and dad know how you're doing."

Grace looked at me with her earnest, large eyes. She was wearing another home-made pink cotton shift, her thin white legs ending in tattered beige Scholl shoes with laces, the kind that old ladies wore. She looked like she was going to cry, but instead, she pressed the pale blue plastic container of her cheesecake into my hands.

"Thanks so much," I said, trying to smile. "I guess I can't return the Tupperware to you this time."

She drew a few deep breaths and nodded. "Oh, it's OK. Thank you for driving all this way to see us. Send my regards to my mother and father."

"I certainly will."

She turned to call her girls to bring Anouk back. We watched the kids bobbing back to us, three little specks of orange against the brown-black wood.

"I thought, he's Christian, so how bad can that be, right?"

I turned to look at her.

Grace was blinking rapidly behind her Coke-bottle glasses. "I just wanted to get married to a Singaporean Christian man and settle down and have a simple life."

That's all. That was all she said, and I just nodded at her, at a loss for words. Then Anouk and I climbed into the SUV, waved once, and roared off.

In the car, Anouk was asking me something. I asked her to repeat her question.

"Are you going to do anything?"

"About?"

"About them! About Melissa and Mindy! We must help them!" Anouk had tears in her voice. "Why can't we do something? Why haven't they run away? Why is she still married to him?"

Parents didn't do well in such moments. Having to explain why evil existed and why it had to be tolerated was worse than having to talk about sex. Far worse. I wasn't even sure if I was qualified for it. The last time a bunch of people sat together to give this question the attention it deserved was in my freshman philosophy class at Brown. I couldn't even remember the outcome of our solemn debate, which seemed to have involved St Augustine. I felt like a cartoon in the *New Yorker*. Something by Roz Chast, a hopeless mother with hair standing up as her kids showered her with questions: *Are you sure carrots are safe? What is dirt made of? If the universe is expanding, why can't I feel it move?*

Why do men beat up their wives and their kids? Why can't the twins wear skirts? Why won't Henry talk to white people? Why can't we save them?

I started to say something about how I used to make judgments about how other people raise their kids, and then I had my own and decided that nobody had a right to judge.

"But Mom, he doesn't even let them wear clothes from the mall!"

"I know. I know. But I'm sure he thinks I'm a real freak for letting you watch *Sex in the City* five nights a week at your age."

"Mom! It's *Sex AND the City*. Anyway, that's different."

"I'm not so sure, honey. Different strokes for different folks."

"But he *beats* them! Aren't you going to do anything?"

Anouk had a troubled expression on her face—a kind of grudging, frustrated humility. This was a situation that she had never prepared herself for and actually didn't know how to react. All her life she had been surrounded by adults whose biggest sins were eating non-dolphin safe tuna and imposing ballet lessons on their daughters. Until we came to Las Vegas, her most recent complaint about parents was that Mrs Hutton, her best friend Angela's mother, dressed "too young for her age" which was "so uncool". To Anouk, the adult world had a big white line dividing down the middle—those who were hip, and those who didn't know how to get with the program. She had difficulty finding where to place Grace and Henry Lee.

Are you going to do anything? It was a moral moment. I had actually thought about all kinds of things I could do. Call the police? Report to social welfare? Call the Singapore Embassy? Call a divorce lawyer? Call

Aunty Lillian and tell her the truth? None of the above were entirely satisfactory. Particularly because Grace and her kids did not specifically ask for help. I wasn't afraid of Henry Lee. I was more afraid of Grace and how there was some complicated equation in her mind which I didn't understand, or have time to dissect, or was even given the permission to do so. And there were two kids in the equation, with a third along the way.

For some reason, my mind drifted from Roz Chast to E. M. Forster, my daughter's hero. There was a story about a man who went out to get his dead sister's baby from a bunch of Italians, and somehow he screwed up, and the baby died. And it all had to do with his inactivity, his moral aloofness, his concern about coming out of the whole affair looking good rather than actually accomplishing anything. He was given a chance to be a good person, to do something. *But it was easier not to.* Life was cleaner that way; you avoided mess. It was a wrenching, empty tale.

The worst thing about being forty is that you feel like you were living the problems of novels that you enjoyed when you were young. You enjoyed them because you thought they were simply about other people's troubles. And their troubles were always so agonizingly pretty and engaging, especially when they made the book into a movie. And then you got to that part of your life and you stop dead and realize those authors weren't kidding and we still didn't have an answer. Maybe Grace had an answer. I remember the cross she wore around her neck.

"I don't know what we should do," I said soberly, looking into the pink distance framed by rusty low hills. "I really don't know and I'm still thinking about it."

Anouk sighed. "OK." Then, "I'm so glad we are going back, Mom."

"Me too." Every mile we were driving was a wedge between them and us. *Go, go, go.* Keep driving. We were heading back to Las Vegas, back to John and back to New York and our things in our apartment and work at the office and Flora our cleaning lady and remembering to use up our season tickets for the Met Opera by the end of the season. Back to a marriage where the biggest problem facing John and myself was controlling our weight from too many late night restaurant meals.

And so we sped on, away from our guilt, and as the miles passed our horror melted away. For a while, we had bristled with righteous indignation and charity, we believed in our potential to be heroic. But only for a while—pragmatism and selfishness was a habit. We convinced ourselves that we were wrong; that people did what they did for a reason; that it was not in our place to judge. As the days passed, as new encounters filled our lives, we lost interest in Grace, Henry, Melissa and Mindy. We forgot that we were ever there, under that roof, in that shooting ranch. The years passed; we went on with our lives. Nothing remained, except for the slightest trace of unease at a lost opportunity.

ACKNOWLEDGEMENTS

What you are holding in your hands would not have reached you but for the enthusiasm of fiction lovers in the countries of Malaysia, Singapore, Ireland and England. Many thanks to Jen Hamilton-Emery at Salt Publishing (UK) and Eric Forbes at MPH Publishing (Malaysia). Thanks to MPH's Janet Tay who fined-tuned the bum notes in the first draft.

English fiction writing in Asia is fueled by grassroots efforts: thank you to Sharon Bakar, for her tireless championing of this cause. I would like to acknowledge the friendship and support given to my recent work by the city of Cork, Ireland, the Munster Literary Centre, the National Library Board of Singapore, and especially the "Cork '08 Gang" of transnational writers and lovers of the short story form: Pat Cotter, Adam Marek, Alison MacLeod, Rob Shearman, Jon Boilard, Julia Van Middlesworth, and Mary O'Donnell.

This volume first appeared in an edition published by MPH Publishing, Kuala Lumpur, in 2007.